The
Dead
Room

Herbert Resnicow

Dodd, Mead & Company
New York

To my daughter, Ruth Anne, with love

Copyright © 1987 by Herbert Resnicow

Published by Dodd, Mead & Company, Inc.
71 Fifth Avenue, New York, N.Y.   10003
Distributed in Canada by
McClelland and Stewart Limited, Toronto
Manufactured in the United States of America

First Edition

1 2 3 4 5 6 7 8 9 10

ISBN 0-396-08982-8

Library of Congress Cataloging-in-Publication Data

Resnicow, Herbert.
The dead room.

I. Title
PS 3568.E69D4   1987   813'.54   86-32977

I

"I couldn't deliver it, Dad," Warren said, "on account of the murder."

That's a reason? I send him out to do a simple little job, a nothing: deliver a list of the new board of directors to Carter Hamilton. Does he do it? No. He has an excuse.

"Who was murdered?" I asked, trying to speak calmly. Warren gets tongue-tied when I yell at him, and right now it was more important to get the whole story than I should try to teach him elementary business communications techniques.

"The inventor," he said. "Walter Kassel."

"Who did I tell you to deliver the list to, Warren?" It was getting harder not to yell.

"The president, Carter Hamilton."

"Was he killed, too, Warren?" What sometimes works is to think of a calm, sunny meadow. With buttercups.

"No, Dad, just Walter Kassel."

"Did Carter Hamilton commit the murder, Warren? Was he arrested?" The meadow wasn't working. Maybe a tropical island with palm trees? Gently swaying?

"I don't think so, Dad. The police haven't arrested anyone yet."

"Then why," the palm trees didn't help, either, "why in hell didn't you deliver the envelope to Carter Hamilton?"

1

Sometimes it's very hard to believe that Warren has a genius IQ.

"I didn't think, with all this trouble, you would have wanted me to give Mr. Hamilton the list."

"You couldn't ask me? All the phones at Hamilcar Hi-Fi suddenly went on the blink?" With his Ph.D. in philosophy, all Warren could do is teach philosophy. But with no jobs for philosophy professors, who's going to study philosophy? Which leads to still fewer jobs for philosophers, which leads to still fewer students, which leads . . . It's a vicious circle and it shouldn't be like that, but it is.

"I thought you'd want to look the situation over, Dad, before you gave Mr. Hamilton the list. You may want to change some names or, if it's still possible, pull out of the deal altogether, now that Mr. Kassel is dead. Let's go there now. I'll drive."

"How was Kassel murdered, Warren?" Working for your father, for Nassau Venture Capital Corporation, Edward Baer, President, is a lot better than working for Burger King, especially if you live at home and type your book all night. Which, if it ever gets published, will be sent free to every philosopher who still has a job. All three of them.

"He was stabbed in the heart, Dad, in the anechoic chamber."

"The dead room?" Skinny as he is (at six feet he should weigh two-twenty, like a man, not one-forty, like a skeleton) Warren didn't flinch at my yell of surprise.

"He was installing the new speaker for testing in the anechoic chamber. When he didn't come out after an hour, the technician went in and found him dead. She called Mr. Hamilton, who called the police."

"When did this happen, Warren?"

"The police say Mr. Kassel was killed about one o'clock, shortly after he entered the anechoic chamber."

"Do they have any idea who did it?"

"No, but it has to be one of the people in Hamilcar Hi-Fi. You know how careful they are about letting in outsiders when they're testing a new product."

"Were all the executives in the building at the time of the murder?"

"Yes, Dad. The police are questioning them now."

"You think they'll be done with Carter Hamilton by the time we get there?"

"If they're not, we can talk to Mr. Gorman or Mr. Borovic first."

"Was the prototype of the new speaker damaged?" I wish Warren would get married already. Maybe Judy Fein? No beauty, but real sharp. Reminds me of Thelma, may she rest in peace. A twenty-five-year-old boy should be a man and not live with his father.

"Only Mr. Kassel was damaged, Dad, not the speaker."

"How could anyone kill anyone in the dead room without being seen by anyone, Warren? It's impossible."

"The body is still in there, Dad. When you talk to the police, you can get all the details."

"Why should I talk to the police, Warren?"

"We have to solve this case, Dad. Fast."

"We? Why we? What do I pay taxes for?"

"Don't you and your golfing buddies have four hundred thousand invested in Hamilcar Hi-Fi already? Aren't you about to invest two hundred thousand more? Do you want the anechoic chamber shut down with the only model of the Kassel speaker in it, until the police find the killer? Which could take weeks? Or more?"

Well, I never said he was completely useless. Maybe if I had pushed him a little more to be a lawyer or an MBA. . . . Even an accountant would have been a big help in the business. But no; Warren had to be stubborn. Warren had to be a doctor of philosophy. In philosophy, yet. One philosophy wasn't enough?

I'll bet that if *I* had delivered that letter, Walter Kassel would be alive today.

II

When that Libyan agent's big brother started pushing the prime rate up to the really big numbers, it was clear to me what was going to happen to the building industry, so I sold my general contracting business fast to a guy to whom things weren't so clear. I accepted the first cash offer I got, which was half what I could have gotten the year before, and I haven't regretted it for a minute since.

Half the money went into tax-exempt bonds, to insure that those fancy muggers in Washington would have to steal from somebody else to get rich, and to make sure that Thelma wouldn't have to remarry for anything but love if I went first. Also so Warren could finish school with a clear head; after that, he was on his own. A little of the rest went into gold, for just in case, and the rest went into growth stocks and warrants. I even took a few small flyers on high-risk speculations just for fun.

Figuring I had my family protected, I looked forward to having more time with Thelma so we could really enjoy ourselves; make up for the years we were working sixteen hours a day building up the business and couldn't spare the time and the money to have a little girl to complete the family. Also it was time I got to know my son better.

After one week Thelma threw me out of the house, saying that if she caught me hanging around driving her crazy after nine and before five, it would be TV dinners for a week straight. "Get a hobby," she told me, "or a girl friend, but stop following me around like a puppy." An occasional lunch together, out of the house, would be fine, provided I sprung it on her and didn't make it a regular deal. Also, she might meet me in town once in a while, for a cocktail before dinner, but to call her an hour in advance so she could doll up.

But you can't suddenly do nothing, after working hard all your life. I went to the temple and the community hospital. They had lots of things for me to do, and I did them, but they were warm-body things, no challenge. One year of that kind of life would absolutely kill me or else turn me into a zombie. I was so desperate that I even thought of going into politics, changing my name so as not to bring shame on my family. Luckily, I did some moaning to Bernie Weber, my dentist, who immediately saved my life. If I wanted challenge, I should join his country club, the Oakdale, one of the finest on the North Shore, right on the Sound, and take up golf. Health and relaxation, he promised me. Also good company, especially Wednesday mornings and Fridays, when all the other dentists and doctors came to get their health and relaxation.

Walking through eighteen holes every day, even when you're with dentists who want to talk only about taxes, is really healthy and relaxing. Golf is not. A game where a skinny, pointy-nosed little runt like Dr. Marvin Guralnik, who never had a muscle in his life, can beat me every time, you can*not* call relaxing. Or healthy.

When I hit the ball, which is usually, it zooms off not less than three hundred yards minimum. And when it goes straight, I can do one over par on the hole, if I don't have too much trouble with my putting. But I can't break a hundred, while Marvin, who plinks a miserable exactly 135 yards per drive and takes three strokes just to get near the green, gets a 96 every time he plays. Never a 95 and never a 97, but exactly a 96. Which shows you the kind of creep he is.

Bernie Weber tells me not to try to kill the ball, but what's the sense of the stupid game if you have a club in your hands and that rotten little ball is just sitting there laughing at you, betting you'll never break a hundred if you live to be two hundred, and you don't use the club to *schlomm* the ball. It's bad to keep emotions bottled up, I read once. Very unhealthy.

Bad as Marvin is, Iris, his wife, is twice. I may be a little heavy; lose twenty pounds, Bob Pasternak says. But Iris is really big, and I don't mean tall; built like a brick brickyard. Iris looks more like a wrestler than a golfer, and not a lady wrestler, either. Five minutes after I met her I offered to bet her she couldn't—it's not that I don't respect women, I do, but Iris has a bigger mouth than even her husband—bet her that she couldn't put the palms of her hands together in front at chest level without bending her elbows. She laughed and told me to eat my heart out; that it was the dream of every man in the club to die smothered to death between her bazooms, and she would play a round with me for a thousand-dollar bet and spot me twenty strokes.

I took her up on it fast, figuring there was no way she could see the ball over her outstanding obstructions, or even hold the club properly. Too fast, really, before I could find out that she was Oakdale's women's champion and shot below eighty. That day she could have shot one-eighty, it wouldn't have mattered, because with her needling, and at needling she was world's champion, period, no sex classification involved whatsoever, with her needling I got lots of healthy exercise climbing in and out of wherever my ball was. When I could find it. I also got very little relaxation that day, before, during, and after the match.

But I shouldn't knock golf, I got my business out of it.

You would think that when educated people like doctors, dentists, lawyers, accountants, businessmen, got together they would discuss art, music, literature, stuff like that. They don't. All you hear is moaning about taxes and how bad the IRS is. I used to join them, in spades, because there is no business that is as strangled by government as construction. One night, when I was telling Thelma about what went on at the club, she told me to stop crying and do something about it.

That's when I got my idea. In the club, all over the country in fact, were people with cash they didn't need to live on, who were working seventy percent for the IRS and thirty percent for their families. Absolute slavery. All over the country there were thousands of other people with energy, drive, ambition, ideas, willing to risk everything, knock themselves out the way I did, to make their dreams come true, but who lacked the money to get started. These people, mostly young, had no way to get the capital; banks don't lend you money unless you have money. I would put the two groups together. I was the ideal guy for this.

I had run a successful business for years; I know the value of a buck and the value of a loyal employee. I had worked with my own hands and had some technical education. Even though I never graduated from Cooper Union, I had passed the very tough entrance exams and had learned something while I was there. I had a good credit rating, some liquid assets, and a good reputation; ask anybody in the construction business about Ed Baer.

The first deal I invested in, I used only my own money. Until I proved myself to myself, I would not ask my friends to risk their money on me. It wasn't a real big deal. A local woman, recently widowed, with four small children, was baking cakes to support the family and was selling them to gourmet restaurants as well as the Oakdale Country Club dining room. Thelma said the cakes were great, the woman was serious, and I had to give her a chance, even if I lost money.

I never went wrong listening to Thelma, so I went to see the baker lady. I was more interested in her than in the numbers. I knew I could make the figures come out good, but I had to know who I was getting into bed with. Not that I expected any problems; anyone who could raise four teenagers, plus run a house and a business single-handed, had to be an all-right type.

It ended up where I put in a wad of money and got fifty percent of the business. I worked with her for three months, setting up the business and the little factory. I retained Irv Waxman, my lawyer, and Monroe Baum, my accountant. We bought a small building and leased out part of it, short term, in case we should need further expansion. I bought professional ovens and equipment, and set up a sales and distribution crew, an advertising agency, and hired a bunch of local ladies, hours adjusted for those who had school-children. I even wrote and copyrighted our slogan: "Ruthanne's Gourmet Cakes—Guaranteed Touched by Human Hands." Would you believe we were in the black seven months after we started production? Ruthanne is now very well off, but she's still supervising every operation herself. And her kids still work in the shop every day after school.

With that success behind me, I formed the Nassau Venture Capital Corporation, which would be the general partner in a series of limited partnerships to be formed; a new one for each new venture.

The limited partnership would get a fifty percent interest in the new company in return for financing and managerial assistance, plus fifty percent representation on the board of directors. The money was put into the corporation in the form of invested capital, long-term loans at the IRS-imputed interest rate, and bank loans guaranteed by the limited partnership. All loans were guaranteed personally by the stockholders of the existing corporation; we were not in the bail-out business, and I wanted the full attention of all the present officers concentrated on making the business work.

The leverage was good, the tax deductions were very good. If we succeeded, if I was right, we made a good profit, helped the economy, and gave some deserving guy a step up the ladder. If he failed, if we lost, our money was tax-deductible, which took some of the sting out of losing, though not the shame.

In my first venture I took in Bob Pasternak, a cardiac specialist; Leonard Vogel and Daniel Tumin, dentists; Bernie Weber, of course; Marvin Guralnik, which I had to do since we played in the same foursome, but it's a mistake to mix business and pleasure if you can call playing golf with Marvin a pleasure; and Jerry Fein, the textile converter with the nice daughter, Judy. The next mistake I made, though it was a good idea at the time, was to give each investor first refusal rights on fifty percent of any new venture of NVC in proportion to his share in the first one.

Nassau Venture Capital Corporation was the general partner in every venture, taking the major risks and getting paid for this. Naturally, as president of NVC, I had a great deal of personal liability and responsibility which, when things were not going too well, and the first year of any new venture is always a money-loser, required a lot of healthy and relaxing walks around the eighteen holes with my regular foursome: me and Fein, Guralnik, and Iris Guralnik. Guess which pair always won.

NVC by now had eight ventures working, of which four were doing very well, two were on the way to breaking even, one was definitely going belly-up, nothing I could do about it now, and one was on the knife edge, could go either way, depending. That one was Hamilcar Hi-Fi Corporation, our latest.

Hamilcar had been founded ten years ago by Carter

Hamilton, a blue-jeans-and-beard dropout from Harvard. With his father's money Hamilton was going to build the perfect acoustic suspension speaker. His handmade model was good enough to lure John Borovic, a promising young engineer, away from his job with another speaker company. Together they produced the prototype model of the HHF-1, which was ten percent smaller than comparable speakers and could be sold for forty dollars less.

Carter recruited his ex-roommate, newly graduated MBA Fred Gorman, to put Hamilcar Hi-Fi together. Fred stole their new sales manager, Roland Franklin, from a retail chain, and got their production manager, Anthony Russo, from a Boston manufacturer. To complete the roster, Fred hired a classmate, the twenty-year-old prodigy, George Sambur, as controller.

Hamilcar made a big splash, spent the money required for a comprehensive and skillful advertising campaign, and expanded rapidly. Too rapidly, in my opinion, but nobody had asked me then. The recession cut sales a little, nothing serious, about ten percent, but with their rapid expansion and their big debt service, the company was in trouble. Carter Hamilton's father died at that time, and his estate turned out to be disappointingly small.

Hamilcar hung on for two years while Hamilton and Borovic were trying to come up with a new model, but by this time, all the possible variations of the acoustic suspension design had been marketed. They finally produced their HHF-2, a cheaply made, cheap-sounding job with a sloppy juke-box bass, which didn't sell well, not even to the rock-and-rollers for whom it had been targeted. The HHF-2 also hurt the previously good reputation of Hamilcar and the HHF-1.

In a desperate attempt to recoup, John Borovic, working night and day, designed the HHF-1A, an improved model of the HHF-1. It was a real good speaker that could be produced for the same price as the HHF-1, but by now the company didn't have enough money or time left to advertise and market the new model properly.

George Sambur, the controller, broke the bad news: In six months they would be bankrupt unless a miracle happened. Sales manager Roland Franklin, normally optimistic, showed them his private projections, which all sloped downward. Fred Gorman, the executive vice president, was given the job, nothing else to do but that, of finding fresh capital; a hopeless prospect, given their present condition, but they were fighters and unwilling to give up.

It was at that time that I explained to Gorman that we were not a bail-out group, or a bunch of liquidators, but were really looking for growth and innovation, neither of which Hamilcar had.

Then the miracle happened. A tall, skinny, wild-eyed old man, shabbily dressed, walked into the Hamilcar offices carrying a package wrapped in brown paper and asked to see the chief salesman. Fortunately, John Borovic was out of town on that day. If Borovic had been there, as he later admitted, he would have thrown the old man out. Once a week an attic inventor comes to a hi-fi company with his latest super-duper creation that either sounds worse than a transistor radio, or else is unpatentable. Speaker design is no longer pure guesswork, cut-and-try; it is now the result of complex computer programs, careful testing, balancing of values, skilled analysis of test results, and inspired engineering by experienced professionals. Sometimes listening to, or even looking at, a civilian's box, lays the company open to lawsuits, especially if the company is working along similar lines itself.

So unless a speaker comes from a person with good credentials and good recommendations, the chief engineer will simply refuse to look or listen. But Rollie Franklin was not the chief engineer, he was a desperate sales manager with his own drooping projections staring him in his soon-to-be-unemployed face. He took Walter Kassel, the old man, into his own office, where he had a good setup to impress buyers, and hooked up the old man's speaker to the left channel of his system. On the right channel Ronnie had dual HHF-1As, which gave very impressive sound. The electronics, naturally, were of the very best kind. Not that Ronnie was a golden ear, but anybody in the trade can tell a great speaker from a good one.

Rollie put a solo piano test record on the turntable and A–B'd the two speakers, the Kassel against the dual HHF-1As, by switching from the left channel to the right, and back again.

The handmade Kassel wiped out the dual HHF-1As as easily as a single HHF-1 had wiped out its competition ten years ago. The little Kassel, smaller than an HHF-2, produced a solid bass that took every low note of the piano with ease. When Rollie closed his eyes, it was as though the piano was in the same room with him.

Trying not to show his excitement, he buzzed Carter Hamilton and asked Carter to step into his office. Carter was just as impressed as Rollie, and even more excited.

There were problems. Kassel had not yet filed his patent application; his patent attorney wouldn't be ready for several months. Kasssel and his lawyer were being extremely careful with the patent claims because a completely new principle was involved. No, Kassel said, he would not disclose the mechanism; if what they heard was not enough, he would go elsewhere. Yes, any nondestructive test could be made, but only by Kassel himself, no one else could touch his speaker. Yes, it could be manufactured by standard machines in any factory. No new technology or manufacturing techniques had to be developed; Kassel was a machinist himself and knew what could be done. In fact, Kessel had made every part of the speaker himself, using only standard tools that could be found in any shop.

It was at that time that Fred Gorman came back to me. Warren was, by then, working with me, and since he was a music lover and I—I loved opera, but when did I have a chance to go?—I did not have as good an ear. We were both impressed by the Kassel speaker and I told Gorman we would reconsider working with them; give me a few days.

One thing about an NVC venture, you get an answer quick, not like with a bank. And since we had already checked their books and everything, all we needed was a meeting of the potential limited partners. This didn't bother me. They always took my recommendations, especially since I invested right along with the others, and my neck was on the line as general partner. Even Marvin Guralnik, who bitched like crazy, even when all went well, would automatically invest his maximum allowable share with me, no matter how hard I tried to talk him out of it.

We had no trouble with my major problem: What if the Patent Office did not grant a patent on the speaker? Kassel had provided the results of three separate searches; no prior art had been uncovered. Of course, looking at prior art patents of loudspeakers meant nothing, since I didn't know what was inside his speaker. Kassel's patent lawyer, Lou Slowicki, was a reputable attorney and he assured Irv Waxman, our attorney, that he found nothing in that prior art that could remotely infringe on the Kassel claims. This did not insure that the patent examiner would not find something that would knock the patent out, but it was good enough for me.

Although we were dying to look at the patent application, and could have done so under a confidential disclosure agreement, Kassel refused. He was a suspicious old man who, he claimed, had been cheated out of another invention when he was young and trusting, and if we didn't believe that what we heard was original, why didn't we check the prior art and copy what was there and make a better speaker ourselves? This didn't sit very well with Hamilton or Borovic, but it didn't kill them either, especially since I was sure they had been doing exactly that for the past few weeks.

Kassel's paranoid secrecy caused us more trouble than even the money negotiations. It was only after Slowicki suggested that the transfer of title to the patent take place right after the filing of the patent application that the impasse was broken. The patent application and agreements for the purchase were placed in escrow with Slowicki, to be released upon filing. That way Kassel retained title until the filing, and we weren't buying a pig in a poke. Our only exposure was the four hundred dollars per week Kassel insisted we pay him to act as consultant during the testing period. This left the Hamilcar people gritting their teeth and dying of curiosity, but it was the only way the deal could be made.

Carter Hamilton was roaring mad that we would have to wait until the filing to see the inside of the Kassel speaker. I had to offer to walk away and let him make his own deal with Kassel before I could get his full attention. He finally agreed that my way was the only way Hamilcar could survive, but I could see that he wasn't highly pleased.

The deal that I finally cut with Hamilcar was that NVC would put in $600,000 in six equal monthly installments; the first $400,000 in secured loans, the rest as pure investment.

Hamilcar was a small, closely held corporation; the executives were the only stockholders. Carter Hamilton had fifty percent, and the other five, Gorman, Franklin, Borovic, Sambur, and Russo, held ten percent each. With us in the picture, getting fifty percent, their numbers were cut in half in proportion. Further, they had to put up their stock as security for all the loans, ours as well as the bank's, which meant that if Hamilcar failed they would all lose their homes, their cars, and their socks. When I'm at risk, everybody I'm in bed with has to have the same incentive to succeed that I have. It wasn't their money I wanted, it was their full, undivided attention to the business of making Hamilcar Hi-Fi a winner. Mistresses, vacations, hobbies, even sleep, had to be put off for a year. Give it your all; that's the only way to win. It was working, too.

NVC meanwhile had been pumping a hundred grand a month into the company. Tony Russo, the production manager, had stopped work on our little lemon, the HHF-2. The price of the remaining stock of the lousy little speakers was reduced to production cost, no markup, and our new ads told the truth: that we had made a mistake and that anyone could pick up a fair second set of speakers for the price of junk. In fact, if you bought a pair of the new improved HHF-1As at the regular price, you got a pair of HHF-2s for one buck. This made Rollie Franklin happy, but it cost plenty. Still, I've always found the first loss is the least loss; if you have to take a licking, take it quick and big, smile, and put your energy to the new sale.

But with Kassel, our new improved genius speaker designer dead, no one knew what our status was, or what Kassel's latest test would look like, or if we could duplicate the product, or even get into the dead room.

But that is now, and I can handle problems like that. No matter what happened to the speaker, or to Hamilcar, I could live through it. Even if this venture lost every penny, we all would live through it. What I wasn't sure I would live through when it happened was . . .

Six months ago everything was perfect. Warren was doing well, his thesis had been accepted with glowing reports. He was even beginning to show me a little respect. NVC was doing very well and I felt happy and productive. Even Iris Guralnik was starting to be nice to me. I had broken a hundred on the course last week and come close to doing it again this week. Thelma was busy with the local Hadassah, just been elected a vice president, and was working mornings with the kids in the leukemia ward of the community hospital.

Thelma was jumpy that morning at breakfast, waiting

for something to happen. "It's not natural for us," she told me, "that things should be so perfect for so long. Something bad is going to happen, I don't know what."

I promised to drive carefully and told her to do the same. She reminded me not to try to kill the ball and to practice an easy swing. I kissed her good-bye.

At nine-thirty Doris Starr, my secretary, came into my office and, without saying a word, poured me a big Scotch from the bottle I keep for guests. I practically don't drink, and never in the morning, but she made me. She then took me in her car, no way she was going to let me drive, to the hospital to identify the body.

It was one of those crazy things, a one-in-a-million chance, but when you're that one, it's a one-hundred-percent-sure thing for you. The police reconstructed it this way: the horizontal railings of the parking building at the hospital were being spray-painted and the little portable air compressor was sitting at the foot of the down ramp on the fourth level. An old lady, driving out of the building, got a heart attack just as she was starting down that ramp and slumped over the wheel with her foot flat on the accelerator. The car hit the air compressor with such force that, when it went between the rails, it flew out eighteen feet to fall exactly on Thelma as she was on her way to the children's leukemia ward. Nobody's fault, really, you couldn't duplicate it in a million years if you tried, but what difference that made, I don't know.

And I wasn't even there to protect her.

Warren came home for the funeral and to stay with me. When the week of mourning was up, he stayed, and maybe that's what kept me alive; to take care of Warren, to see him married, to see Thelma's and my grandchildren, that was worth living for.

So there we were: the empty little family in the big empty house: Ed Baer, big-deal venture capitalist, and my son, the philosopher.

III

Fred Gorman got right to the point. "I hope this unfortunate event won't change our relationship, Mr. Baer." The executive vice president of Hamilcar looked like what J. Edgar Hoover would have liked all his G-men to look like. Fred was tall, slim, blond, and boyish, with light blue eyes behind rimless glasses, looking too young to be an executive of anything bigger than a lemonade stand. I'd gotten used to that; all the new hi-tech companies are run by adolescents, practically, and we old fogies are the ones who are out of place. But Fred had a sharp brain behind that movie-actor face, and he worked as though his life depended on the success of the company, which maybe it did, so I forgave him his looks.

"Why shouldn't it change our relationship, Fred?" I asked. "Without the Kassel speaker, Hamilcar isn't going anywhere."

Fred's office was . . . I guess smooth is the word. The carpet was brown and the beige walls displayed a few small engravings of scenes of Old London. On his dark oak desk everything was in order: telephone on the right, notepad on the left, pen-and-clock set centered. His "in" box was empty; his "out" box was full. His dark blue suit fit perfectly into the office; any rising young executive could have moved into either the office or the suit without changing a thing.

"I can name you twenty other good speakers in the one A's price range, Fred. Without the Kassel, Hamilcar doesn't warrant any more money dumped into it."

"If you don't put in the other two hundred thousand, Mr. Baer," he pointed out calmly, "you'll lose the four hundred you already invested."

I brought him down fast. "Lent, Fred, not invested. Only the last two hundred gets invested. And you guys are on the hook for the loans personally. I think there's enough asset between the plant and the personal holdings of you six to let us walk out almost clean." And just to make sure he got the point, I added, "That is, if we do it right now, and don't wait."

Fred looked at me shrewdly. "Why are you talking that way, Mr. Baer? To crack the whip? That doesn't sound like you."

"Exactly, Fred, to crack the whip. And it sounds *just* like me, when I'm about to lose my investors' money." It was good he got the picture so quickly, but I would have been happier if he had been ahead of me.

"You don't really want to close us down, do you?"

"No, but I will if I have to."

"What do you want me to do, Mr. Baer?"

"If you have to ask, should you be the executive vice president of a possibly growing company?"

"There was no way for me to get that speaker before the police came. You can't just zip in and out of the anechoic chamber."

"Take me there," I said, standing up. "Show it to me."

"Sit down, Mr. Baer," Fred said. "The police have sealed the room."

"There's only one way to get in?"

"Two, but there's a cop in front of each door. Besides, you can't get to the speaker from the lower entrance."

"Why not?" I asked, sitting down.

Gorman settled back in his swivel chair and put his fingertips together. "Any good speaker company has an anechoic chamber, a place without echoes, in which it tests its products. It's important to eliminate resonances, external noise, any sound other than that produced by the speaker being tested."

"That's why you call it the dead room?"

"Our anechoic chamber is as acoustically dead as a room can be. Carter and John designed it when we built the plant."

"They didn't like the regular type of chamber? What's so special about ours?"

"Our anechoic chamber is a huge concrete box, thirty feet wide inside as you enter it, forty feet high, and fifty feet deep."

"That sounds like there'd be a lot of echoes," Warren said.

"No two walls are parallel," Fred replied, "and every surface is covered with sound traps, stiff wire mesh rolled into five-foot-long cylinders with the open ends facing into the room. The cylinders are filled with lamb's wool held in place with cheesecloth."

"So it's like the inside of a cow's stomach," I said. "Tripe. But if the whole inside is covered with sound cylinders, where do you test the speakers?"

"Halfway up there's a reinforced concrete beam jutting out from the rear wall. It holds a jig to which the speaker is bolted, and the beam is covered with lamb's wool, too, so that there are no hard surfaces to reflect sound."

"You can't cover the light fixtures," I pointed out. "They have to reflect sound."

"No light fixtures. The microphone doesn't have to see and no one can be in the chamber while the test is on."

"What about the guy who bolts the speaker on the test jig? He has to see."

"He brings in a photographer's light tripod and takes it out when he's done."

"What does he stand on? And the lights?"

"Halfway up the chamber a net is stretched across the entire area. It's made of soft rope in six-inch squares, and it's a little slack so it doesn't vibrate."

"Like a trapeze safety net?" I asked. "Then how do you walk on it?"

"It's tighter than a safety net; just sags a bit where you step on it. If you were very careful you could walk on it with regular shoes, but we have a better way. Snowshoes."

"Real snowshoes?"

"Actually, pieces of plywood with a spongy sole glued on. Strap them on your feet and you can walk on the net, although it's a bit clumsy. We always keep a few sets in the airlock."

"A real airlock?"

"That's what we call it. It's just the vestibule outside the chamber door."

Warren was looking anxious, so I let him talk. "You said, Mr. Gorman, that the anechoic chamber is a big room with a net floor halfway up." Fred nodded his handsome blond head. "And the inside of the chamber is covered with sound-trap cylinders?" Fred nodded again. "So how do you get from the vestibule, airlock, into the chamber?"

"Imagine you're standing inside the airlock. Directly in front of you is the door to the dead room. Pull open the door and you're looking at the back end of a bank of sound trap cylinders that are fixed together and slide on rails. Push this assembly in and you can go into the chamber. When you've finished installing the speaker, pull the assembly back into position, close the door, and you're ready to test."

"How big is the vestibule?" Warren asked.

"Above five feet square."

"And the light tripod is in it? And snowshoes? And the doors open inward? Sounds crowded, Mr. Gorman."

"Somewhat," Fred admitted, "but it's big enough."

"Wait," I said. "Why doesn't the light tripod fall through the netting?"

"It stands on a plywood base," Fred said. "If you don't jiggle around, it's quite stable."

"Was Kassel's body on the netting?"

"So I understand." Fred was beginning to look irritated.

"Who found the body?"

"Janie Zausmer, the testing technician. Kassel should have been in there fifteen minutes or less. When he didn't come out after an hour, she went in to look."

"Why didn't she just plug a mike into the speaker inputs and talk to him on the test speaker?"

"You never do that." Gorman looked shocked. "You don't know what's going on in there. You could blow the speaker if you used it at the wrong time."

It was time to get down to business. "Did you see anyone around the airlock, Fred, about the time Kassel was killed?"

He twitched. "What makes you think I was near the airlock at that time?" I just looked at him. "All right, Mr. Baer. I was dying to know how the test was going. You would have done the same."

I ignored that last part. "Who else was hanging around the airlock?"

"On the first floor, Borovic, Sambur, and Franklin. In the basement, Russo."

"Why did you go down to the basement, Fred?"

"I didn't want the assembly people to know how nervous I was. I couldn't hang around the testing area all the time."

"You didn't see Hamilton?"

"We must have missed each other. I'm sure he was as concerned as I was."

I suddenly realized what I disliked about Fred Gorman. Outside of his looks, I mean. Whenever he got a chance, he would take a subtle, very subtle, dig at Carter Hamilton. So I put it on the table, in plain English. "What have you got against Hamilton, Fred?"

He looked shocked. I guess in his circle you're not supposed to be so crude as to ask anything directly. Tough on his circle, then. I waited, looking him straight in the eye.

"I don't have anything against Carter personally, now," he said slowly. Probably figured, as long as it was out, take advantage of the situation and score some points with the majority stockholder.

I was willing. In fact, I was anxious to learn, so I picked up the ball. "You have professional disagreements?"

He pulled back a bit. "I always followed company policy exactly, Mr. Baer, once it was established, regardless of personal feelings. I implemented Carter's decisions efficiently."

That I believed, although Eichmann had put it better. "Did you express your disagreements? Like at the board of directors' meetings?"

"No. Only to Carter privately. I didn't want to show dissension in front of the others."

I'll bet. That way he could share the credit if Carter was right, and claim foresight if Carter was wrong. I put the words in his month. "Building the HHF-2, for instance?"

"That was one of the most important mistakes he made. I told him it would change our image, and the results proved me right."

I didn't need any more, but just in case Nassau Venture Capital didn't pull the plug, and just in case Hamilcar needed a new president in the near future, for whatever reason, such as the old one being in the clink, I laid it on the line. It wasn't the answer that I needed, that I already knew, guaranteed, but *how* he answered, that was what counted. "I take it you have plans on how to run the company better, if you get the opportunity?"

This time *he* looked *me* straight in the eye. "In writing," he said flatly.

Good. He may have been a sneaky bastard, but he was a *smart,* sneaky bastard, and he had balls enough to take major risks when the chips were down. He'd make a good president someday. If he wasn't the killer, that is. "Let's get back to the dead room, Fred," I said. "Is the net at the same level as the airlock floor?"

"At the door, yes. In the middle, it sags a little."

"And in the basement, the tops of the sound-trap cylinders, they're also at the vestibule level?"

"Yes, the concrete box is sunk into the ground."

"From what you said, the net must be fifteen feet above the tops of the cylinders. Are snowshoes kept in the lower airlock, too?"

"No, no one ever uses that door; it's only for repairs. If any work has to be done down there, you bring in sheets of plywood to stand on." He took off his glasses and looked me in the eye again; he sure knew how to use the sincere look. I guess they teach that to MBAs these days. "And no plywood is kept in the plant if that's what you're hinting, Mr. Baer; we buy our cabinets assembled."

"Couldn't a man walk on top of the wire-mesh cylinders?"

"If he had a light and walked slowly and carefully, watched where he put his feet, yes, it could be done. What are you thinking of? That somebody went in there to kill Kassel? That's impossible."

To a guy like Fred, nothing is impossible, so I pressed on. "A pole with a knife attached, maybe? You said the net floor has holes in it six inches square."

"Would you like to bring a twenty-foot pole," he asked, "into a dark room, holding a flashlight in your teeth, walking on the edge of wire-mesh cylinders—or even with snowshoes—and try to stab someone through the heart through a six-inch hole? Lots of luck, Baer." His perfect control had slipped enough to make him forget to call me "Mr." I must have touched a nerve somewhere.

"Are there people working near the basement airlock?" I asked.

"Warehouse crew, but they're there to work, not to watch doors." Fred looked very agitated.

"I'd like to talk to Janie Zausmer now," I told him.

"I'll have her meet you at the test console," Fred said, putting his glasses on again. I guess the time for sincere looks was over. "My secretary will give you directions."

Warren and I spoke as we walked. "It seems," Warren said, "there is no way Kassel could have been killed. Yet he was. There must be some simple explanation."

"So put your expensively trained Ph.D. mind to work," I said. "For what eight years at Yale cost me, you should have the answer already."

"I made the terrible mistake," he replied, "of studying philosophy instead of criminology. But why haven't you come up with the solution, Dad? Considering that you were in the construction business, you must be more familiar with violence than I am."

"Don't get fresh, Warren. I never did business with those people and you know it. And I never studied criminology either, but I bet you the minute I get inside the chamber I'll figure out how it was done. I'm good at things like that. Ask anybody."

"The way Kassel was killed is not the key. What interests me more is why he was killed. The first thing to ask is: *Cui bono?* What is the good? Who gains?"

I always knew he wasn't stupid, but I didn't expect him, right out of school, to be so practical either. Good genes will tell; the ones he got from Thelma, may she rest in peace. But from where he got his big mouth, I don't know. Certainly not from me.

Well, no sense in fighting now; I'd straighten him out later. "As far as we know," I said, "nobody gains. In fact, everybody loses, us included. Let's see what Janie has to say."

IV

Janie Zausmer hadn't gotten to the test area yet, so we took the opportunity to look around. Seated at the test console, the entrance to the airlock was twenty feet to the left. Concentrating on the knobs and dials, Janie could have seen the airlock door only peripherally. The assembly crew nearby was concentrating on its work.

I could have sneaked an army, one by one, into the dead room and no one would have noticed. If it weren't for the cop guarding the door, Warren and I could have gone in and checked the scene of the crime ourselves. And, incidentally, taken the Kassel speaker home with us and reduced the amount of sweating in both Hamilcar and Nassau Venture Capital.

Janie was a plump little middle-aged woman dressed in a white smock. "The inspection area where I usually work is at the other end of the plant," she apologized.

"Then you're not normally stationed here?" Warren asked.

"Only when there's a test to be run. I come here to turn on the equipment to warm it up before the test and wait for whoever is installing the speaker—usually it's Mr. Borovic—to come out and tell me everything is ready."

"This time it was Mr. Kassel?"

"He's a lot slower than Mr. Borovic. He's an old man and the test rig is high up, so I knew he would take a long time. That's why I went to the ladies' room then, otherwise I wouldn't be able to go during the testing. Mr. Kassel took a long time with the tests; everything had to be done over and over."

"When did you leave the console?"

"Right after lunch, about a quarter after one."

"What if Kassel needed you while you were gone?"

"Before I went I turned up the mike output so the assemblers could hear. If Mr. Kassel wanted anything while he was in the chamber, one of the girls would come and get me."

"So you could hear everything that goes on in the chamber?"

"Oh, sure. It's a very sensitive mike."

"Did you hear anything suspicious?"

"When he first went in I heard a few grunts, like. The rig is up high and I guess lifting a speaker up and sliding it on the bolts is hard for an old man, especially standing on the netting."

"Did you hear anything when you came back from the ladies' room?"

"No, sir, but that's normal. I keep the gain low so if he should say anything near the mike I wouldn't get my ears blasted off."

"Show me how you sit, Mrs. Zausmer."

She pulled the chair close to the console and put on a pair of glasses. She leaned forward and turned knobs with her left hand and made writing motions with her right. "I adjust the signal generator, calibrate the mike, and take readings at the mike locations and distances the test calls for."

"Which tests were you going to run today?"

"The last test, transient response on-axis at one meter, at one-third octave frequencies."

"I see you use reading glasses," I said.

"Only for close work, sir. At my age, I'm beginning to need a little help."

"So even if you have seen someone going into the dead room or coming out, you couldn't have identified him?"

"I didn't see anybody, but I think I could. It isn't just the face, you know, that lets you recognize people. But I really wasn't watching. I didn't expect . . ."

"Why did you wait so long before you went into the chamber, Mrs. Zausmer?"

"I don't like to disturb the executives. Sometimes Mr. Borovic is very irritable, especially when a test isn't going right. He says my job is to sit at the console and I get paid by the hour so to mind my own business. But it was an hour, sir, and that's too long."

"So you went into the chamber?"

"Just to check up. I looked in—"

I interrupted, "Did you open the inner door and push in the rack of sound-trap cylinders?"

"I didn't have to, sir. The inner door is always left open; the plug for the lights is in the airlock. There's no point in pulling back the cylinders until you're ready to make the test. It's double work otherwise."

"Then anyone who opened the outer door could see Kassel being killed?"

"Not really, sir. The sound-absorbing cylinders are in the way between the inside door and the test rig. When you go in you have to step left and then right again, around the bank of sound absorbers."

"So you walked into the chamber and saw Kassel dead?"

"I put on the snowshoes and went in. The knife was in his chest and his smock was covered with blood."

"You didn't go near him?"

"I was afraid to. He wasn't moving. I knew he was dead."

"Describe what you saw, please, Mrs. Zausmer."

"It's like I told the police. Mr. Kassel was flat on his back, right in front of the test rig. The light rig was lying flat on the net near him, on his left, sort of parallel to him.

It was horrible. There was blood all over the front of his smock."

"What was the position of his arms and legs?"

"His arms were stretched out sideways, his legs were straight out, a little up in the air on account of the snow-shoes."

"He was still wearing the snowshoes?"

"They're strapped on; you couldn't walk on the netting without them very easily."

"But it could be done, couldn't it?"

"I'm sure it could, sir, by a young man with good balance and good eyes."

"Relax," I said, "I'm not accusing you. Do the police think you did it?"

"They know better. Why should I? I've lived in Oakville all my life and never gave any trouble and my nephew is a sergeant in the Nassau County Police."

"What angle was the knife?"

"Straight up, sir."

"As though it had been pushed in," I asked carefully, "from the front, rather than stabbed downward? Like this?" I made a stabbing motion downward toward her. "Or upward, from below?" I reversed my hand and stabbed upward, but what I really had in mind was still the pole from below.

"No, sir, it was straight in, the way you said, like it was pushed, not stabbed."

"Thank you, Mrs. Zausmer," I said. "You've been very helpful."

"Wait a minute, Dad," Warren said. "I'd like to ask a few questions." He turned to Janie Zausmer. "There are no lights in the chamber. How could you see so clearly if the light tripod was knocked over?"

"The lights are on arms sticking out from the pole, sir, and the rig was rolled toward Mr. Kassel. There was plenty of light on him."

"How far from him were the lights? How far from the test stand was he?"

"The lights were about five feet to his left and his feet were about a foot away from the test stand."

That was that, so he let her go. "I'd like to see the inside of that chamber," I said, "so I can figure out *how* Kassel was killed."

"So would I," Warren said. "It may give me an idea as to *why* he was killed." Still stubborn, as usual, but I was too polite to say anything right now.

The lower entrance to the anechoic chamber was in the warehousing area, where the cartons of speakers were stacked. With their usual intelligence and attention to detail, Hamilcar had set up adjustable perforated-strut supports for three levels of framed steel-mesh shelving: one just above floor level, one about six feet up, and the top one another six feet above that.

Narrow aluminum ladders, a foot wide, with hooks fixed to the top end, hung vertically from the top shelves here and there, completely out of the way of the platform trucks being pushed up and down the narrow aisles, and yet available to be moved where needed easily and quickly.

The entrance to the lower airlock was at the far end of the third aisle from the last; you had to press a switch at the beginning of the aisle to turn the lights on full, more money saving I was pleased to see, although the workmen seemed not to bother, their eyes accustomed to the dimmer light. There was a cop standing in front of the door who politely asked us who we were, and who was under orders to let no one in. He didn't know when the detective in charge, Sergeant Palmieri, would allow use of the room again, but he was sure it would be several days, at least.

I decided to see if Carter Hamilton was finished talking to the police.

V

In certain industries—electronics, computers, hi-fi—huge organizations are run by kids who, if you see them, you wouldn't trust to run a peanut stand. Hamilcar Hi-Fi was no exception. Short, skinny Carter Hamilton, president and chairman of the board, had a neat little pigtail and a skimpy beard. He wore expensive jogging shoes, custom-tailored blue-denim overalls, and a fitted brushed-cotton khaki shirt. How his overalls became worn I'll never know; he certainly never worked with his hands a day in his life. Maybe Brooks Brothers will sandpaper clothes for a price. When an executive wears work clothes it doesn't mean the guy is stupid or incompetent. What it does show is that he doesn't want to play by the existing rules. However marginally this reduces the confidence of bankers, credit managers, and subcontractors, whoever you do business with, it isn't worth whatever the gain is to your ego. It usually pays to put on the uniform for just that one day and give the right passwords. In business you don't neglect any advantage, no matter how small. When I used to go to the bank for a mortgage or a construction loan, I always put on my "bank suit," a pin-striped navy blue, with a white cotton shirt and a small-figured tie. Although I practically never wore a tie any other time, it didn't kill me to put one on twice a year.

If you want to be true to yourself, and you really are a

poor farmer, okay. But no one would have mistaken Carter
Hamilton, Aristocrat Second Class, with his baby-blue
eyes, thin sandy hair, and soft body, for a poor, hard-
working black Southern sharecropper, no matter what he
wore.

On the walls of his office Carter kept a running exhibi-
tion of nature pictures: waterfalls, forests, and mountains,
plus very-close-up shots of flowers and insects. Very well
done they were, too; really professional, you could tell
where his heart was. But what wasn't there was people,
not one shot, not even of Betsy Collins, the girl he lived
with since his last year of college. A real nice girl, I met her
a few times. Why they didn't get married and have a family, I'll never know. I would have felt better about him,
personally as well as businesswise, if Carter had some pictures of kids on the wall, his kids, and not just nature.

I noticed that he didn't have even one picture of a calm,
sunny meadow, with buttercups. Or a tropical island with
palm trees, gently swaying.

Seeing how harassed he looked, I made soft, soothing
noises for a minute—a little hand holding never hurts with
certain types—then got down to business. "What do you
intend to do now, Carter?" I asked.

"Get the police removed so we can get back to work on
the new speaker," he snapped.

"How will you do that, Carter?"

"As soon as they finish the photography and measure-
ments I'm going to tell the chief to unseal the anechoic
chamber. John has to complete the testing so we can put all
the results together and analyze them. Then we have to
adjust the mechanical and electrical elements to optimize
the performance."

"Open the Kassel speaker, you mean?"

"I don't think we should use that name anymore," he
said. "I think the HHF-10 would be better."

"To give the idea," I smiled sweetly, "that Hamilcar's

brilliant Carter Hamilton, ably assisted by the almost-as-brilliant John Borovic has, after years of struggle and flashes of genius, finally produced the speaker of the century?"

He didn't blush. "Precisely," he said. "Tell me, Baer, do they call it the 'Carlsen,' 'Haloid,' or 'Xerox'?"

"That's a good point, Carter, but I still don't like the name HHF-10." It was time to stick in the needle and see what came out. "HHF-10 sounds too much like HHF-2. However did you allow that piece of junk to get built?"

His face grew red. "That was a sound decision at the time, Baer. We couldn't keep going much longer with only one product line; we had to break into a low-price, high-volume market."

"Yeah," I retorted, "just in time when the rockers began to demand good sound. A brilliant administrative decision you made."

"We had no way of knowing they would develop golden ears at that time. And it wasn't only my decision. We all agreed."

"You were the president; you could have stopped it."

"I'm not the only one, Baer. That was a real stupid deal you made with Kassel." Carter pressed on. "Can you imagine, at this stage, with the company's life depending on this one product, we still don't know even the operating principle? We should have insisted that he disclose the design before we paid him one penny."

"All we've paid him, so far, is four hundred dollars per week," I reminded Carter. "Kassel was ready to walk, I could tell. You were pretty anxious to get the speaker for Hamilcar yourself, I remember, really drooling."

"Things have changed, Baer. Now that Kassel isn't around to stymie my every move, I can do what's best for the company." He stroked his little beard complacently.

"I wouldn't advertise that Kassel's death was a godsend to the company, Carter," I advised. "It might give the police some wrong ideas."

"They know I didn't do it. I don't see why I shouldn't take advantage of the opportunity."

I thought I knew what he meant, but I had to make sure. "Are you suggesting, Carter, that as soon as the police let us into the dead room, we take apart the speaker and steal the design?"

"Why pay upfront money and royalties unnecessarily?"

I tried to talk calmly. "Because we made a deal, Carter. Because we negotiated the terms and shook hands. Because we deal straight, that's why." And because the guy who tries to screw others, I didn't say it out loud, is the guy who will, some day, try to screw his own partners.

"I've already called Waxman and asked him to look into it. We'll talk about it after he gives his legal opinion."

"I'm surprised he didn't spit in your eye over the phone, Carter. If he says we can legally take the design, which I doubt, you just haven't thought things through yet. I'll stop you at the board of directors' meeting. If Kassel has any heirs, they're entitled to the inheritance."

"Kassel has no heirs; he told me. Do you want to give the speaker to the state?"

"I want to do what's right, Carter; that's how we do business. We accepted the deal, we were satisfied with it, and we're going to live by our word."

"I'm president of Hamilcar," he stood up and jabbed his finger at me, "and I decide what we do, not you." Some small men have to act big, I guess.

I leaned back in my chair and smiled. I had gotten worse from guys a lot tougher than Hamilton, so I wasn't exactly trembling with fear. "After you decide what to do, Mr. President, what are you going to do it with? If I don't put in my hundred grand on the first, you can't even make payroll."

I thought he was going to bust open, but he took a deep breath and sat down. He spoke quietly, no finger pointing now. "You have a contractual obligation, Mr. Baer, to put in the money as agreed."

"And you, Mr. Hamilton," I replied, "have a contractual obligation to produce the Kassel speaker on time and within the money I'm putting in. If you don't keep your end of the bargain, why should I keep mine?"

"You break the contract, Mr. Baer, and I'll sue NVC and you personally, as general partner."

I knew I had won. "Do that, Carter. In about ten years, if you live that long on a food-stamp diet, we'll meet in court. Assuming you can afford the lawyer's fees."

He changed tack. "My way, we'll get the speaker produced on time."

"Your way stinks, Carter. I want you to do it the right way. It can be done, if you'll just put your mind to it instead of spending time and energy trying to figure out how to get around the Kassel agreement."

He got red again. "Anytime you don't like the way I run this company, Mr. Baer, you can pull out. Given enough notice, I'm sure I can get you your money back. With interest."

"You mean now that you have the speaker all to yourself? Think again, Carter. You don't have the speaker for free. We have signed agreements with Kassel that we are going to honor. And you can't throw my crew out; don't even think of it. You try, and I'll tie you up so tight you won't be able to go to the toilet without a court order, much less touch the speaker. And I'll give you one more bit of advice. Don't threaten; do. A threat just confuses me. I don't know if you're talking this way because you're upset or because you really intend to do something bad. So I'll wait and see. If you attack me, then I know what to do. And I'll teach you something else, sonny. If you really want to attack someone, shoot to kill. And do it in the dark, from behind, with your mouth shut. Like maybe you did with Kassel."

"Are you accusing me of killing Kassel?"

"Did you? Where were you between one and two today?"

"In the plant. Around. I don't know exactly where."

"Did anyone see you?"

"How the hell do I know? And why are you questioning me? Do you really think I did it?"

"No outsider was in the plant. And I don't think some poor schnook from the loading dock had anything to gain from killing Kassel. So it had to be you, or one of your execs, someone who felt he had something to gain by the murder. And I'll find out who."

"You? Why? What do you know about something like this?"

"I've been faced with all kinds of problems in my day, Carter. Big ones. I've solved most of them and I'm still here. Practically all problems in business boil down in the end to money or personalities; I understand both. The quickest way to get Hamilcar back in full operation, and to protect my investment, is to solve the murder. As for why—because I don't want to be partners with a killer. Once he gets used to solving his personal problems with a knife, he might decide that I'm hampering the way he's running the company. Or that Warren is in his way. I'm not going to live that way, always wondering which of my partners is going to knock me off. And if it's you, Carter, I'll turn you in as fast as any mugger. We can always get a new president if we have to. He might even be an improvement. Good-bye." Hamilton was shaking as we left. I guess no one had ever spoken to him this way before, and maybe it would do him some good. I hoped it would; he had enough good qualities to be worth saving. I slammed the door for emphasis.

"Why were you so rough on him?" Warren asked. "You shouldn't talk to the president of Hamilcar that way."

"Don't tell me how to talk, Warren. I knew how to talk to presidents when you were still peeing in your diapers."

"I've heard you treat laborers with more respect."

"When they earn it, they get the respect. Besides, I wasn't any harder on him than I've been on you."

"Exactly," he said, with a look. I was ready to explain to him that it was for his own good, to teach him what's what, when he changed the subject. "You don't really think he did it, do you? He doesn't seem to be the type."

"Everybody's the type; don't let that hippie getup fool you. Everybody can kill, even me and thee, under the right conditions. I just like to think that for me the conditions are very limited. Like to save my life. Or yours. Or any human's. But you never know."

"I think you're right about it being one of the execs," Warren said, "but I don't see how anyone gains. Even if Mr. Hamilton steals the invention, it doesn't make that much difference financially."

"It does for Carter. He now has twenty-five percent of the stock. A quarter of what Kassel would have gotten may not be big, but it's not negligible. Still, we shouldn't close our minds to other motives. People don't kill only for money. There's hate and love and revenge and lots of other things."

"We could check into Kassel's private life."

"We will, later. First I'd like to talk to Kassel's patent lawyer, Lou Slowicki. What time is it?"

"It's only four-thirty. I'll call and ask if he can see us now."

"I'll make a call, too. I want to acquaint our limited partners in Hamilcar Venture Associates of the facts. We'll meet in my office tonight at eight. You should be there, too, Warren."

Slowicki was in his office in Mineola, only fifteen minutes away. He'd wait for us. Irv Waxman said he'd call all the limited partners. I wondered if I'd done the right thing, fighting with Carter Hamilton at this time. I wish I had Thelma to talk things over with; she always knew what to do. Warren might be smart, but he had no experience. Well, he'd just have to do.

VI

The courtly old attorney toyed with the rimless glasses hanging on the ribbon around his neck. "Yes," Slowicki said, "there will be some complications, but Waxman and I can work things out."

"The main question," I said, "is can Hamilcar proceed with the patent application for the speaker?"

Slowicki thought for a moment, then said, "The intent and the letter of the escrow agreement were that title to the patent would be transferred to Hamilcar upon filing. I feel it is consistent with the agreement and in the best interests of all parties that an officer of Hamilcar sign the patent application just prior to filing and that I release the escrowed material immediately after filing."

"When will that be?"

"We intended to file in about two weeks, depending on how big the changes required by Mr. Kassel would be, if any. He seemed pretty confident that the tests would work out well and no changes would be required."

"Lou"—I was acting a lot more casual than I felt—"under these conditions, how about disclosing the patent application to us?"

"I'm sorry," he said, and I think he meant it, "I can't. The terms of the escrow agreement are very specific. There is no way I can breach the agreement."

Well, no one can say I didn't try. On to another matter.

"Tell me again, Counselor, that this one is sure to be granted a patent."

"I can't tell you that, Mr. Baer, but I will repeat what I told Waxman. I have been in this profession for forty years and, within the limits of my knowledge and according to three separate searches made by a reputable Washington firm I have dealt with for twenty years, there seems to be no prior art that conflicts or interferes with the Kassel invention. Further, the approach is along significantly different lines from anything in the prior art. This does not mean that the patent examiner will not find some reason to refuse the patent, but I consider it highly likely that a patent will be issued and that it will grant at least one of our broader claims in substantially the same language it is in now."

"That's good enough for me, Mr. Slowicki. What changes will you have to make in the application?"

"Under the present circumstances, none. Mr. Kassel will not be making any changes and Hamilcar is unable to request any change since Mr. Borovic doesn't know what is inside the black box. All I have to do is put everything in its final form, proofread the application, and get Mr. Hamilton's signature. One week should do it."

"Can Kassel's heirs make any difficulties?"

"From the way he spoke, I don't think he has any heirs and, I venture to say, he died intestate."

"How does that affect Hamilcar?"

"Not at all, Mr. Baer. You will make all required payments to me as per agreement, to be placed in escrow for any potential claimant. If no will turns up, the state will become, in effect, the heir, and will claim all monies, less fees and costs."

"What about royalties, directorship, Kassel's professional consultation fees?"

"No real problem. The state is not interested in risks or in being a director. I'm sure that a relatively low lump-sum settlement will be acceptable for release of all their claims. As for Kassel's fees, they were for services to be performed. No services, no fees required. Hamilcar can, and should, be able to continue functioning as though nothing had happened in terms of doing business."

"It's a pleasure dealing with you, Mr. Slowicki," I said. "Most other lawyers would have taken two hours of ands, ifs, and buts to give me the same information. Just one more thing: Did Kassel ever mention any enemies to you? Anyone who might have wanted to do him harm?"

"None, Mr. Baer. But he acted very furtively, secretive. He wanted assurances that I would not steal his invention or show it to anyone. That's why I gave Waxman such a hard time on no one's seeing the application until it was filed, not even under a confidential disclosure agreement."

"Isn't that unusual?"

"Very. But Kassel was unusual in every way. Nothing was to be mailed, nothing discussed. I gave him the searches, he took them home and studied them and came back a few days later with typed comments. Hardly said a word, just handed me the papers. Wouldn't even leave them with my secretary. He picked up the first draft of the application himself and brought it back a few days later with a list of corrections, typed out, probably with one finger. No mistakes, everything very neat. A real obsessive personality, but I guess all machinists are that way, especially old-time Europeans."

"He wasn't American born?"

"I think not. Or maybe he came from the Penn Dutch country; he had that kind of slight accent. He was also a very skillful freehand sketcher."

"Was he still working, at his age?"

"Not really. He was on Social Security, but I'm sure he did odd machinist jobs here and there off the books. Most skilled craftsmen augment their income that way; it's very hard to live on Social Security these days."

"Do you know where he lived?"

"He had a room a few blocks from here, with an old Irish lady who gave him breakfast and supper. I phoned him there whenever there was anything for him to pick up."

"Do you know her well enough to ask her to let us see his room?"

"I do, but I'm not sure I should. Why?"

"My problems will be a lot easier, and Hamilcar's, too, if Kassel's killer is caught very soon. I'd like to do whatever I can to help the police catch him."

"Playing detective, eh? Sounds like fun. I can't let you go through his things, Mr. Baer; I may very well end up as executor. But I'll go with you if you promise not to pick anything up without my knowledge."

I agreed. Why not? Mrs. Dolan told Slowicki on the phone that the police had been there already and that she would put up tea for us. I decided to pick up a tin of Danish butter cookies on the way. Poor old ladies get very upset if there is nothing in the house to offer guests.

VII

"No," Mrs. Dolan said, "he never gave any trouble. Hardly said a word or made a sound. Just stayed in his room all day watching TV." The tea was very strong, the way I like it, and the cookies were perfect with them. The little red-faced old lady fussed over Warren; skinny boys bring out the mother in them all, and made him eat extra cookies. With the pride of the poor, she wanted me to take the leftover cookies home, but I refused.

Upstairs, Kassel's room was spare, almost bare. A bed, a chair, a table with a Bible on it, a carton of Winstons, a lamp, a clock radio, a TV, some clothes, and a worn leather case with a perfectly oiled set of micrometers. That's it. A whole life, nothing to show.

We checked through the drawers and his clothes. Nothing. The police, Mrs. Dolan said, hadn't found anything, either.

"Did Mr. Kassel have any relatives?" Warren asked. "Or any visitors?"

"None at all," Mrs. Dolan said. "A lonely man he was; you'd hardly know he was in the house at all."

"Did he receive letters? Phone calls? Any contact with others?"

"Only his checks, poor soul. And sometimes calls for work, from Mr. Tinopolis and another gentleman. And from Mr. Slowicki."

"Did he say anything to you about his invention?"

"Once he said he was going to be rich soon, but he never told me how. I didn't believe him; dreams, you know, we all have them. I used to have such dreams before . . . before. Was it true?"

"Not rich," I said, "but he would have had a nice lump of money and an income. For him, it might have seemed like riches. Did he have any other source of income, Mrs. Dolan? That you know of?"

She looked a bit guilty. "Well, the Social Security, it isn't hardly enough, you know. I suppose it doesn't matter now, what with him dead and all, but he used to pick up a bit nights now and then at the place down in Westbury. Had to take the bus at the depot."

"Working for one of the men you mentioned before?"

"The Greek, it was. Tinopolis or something. And sometimes the other one, in the past year or so. He was a good machinist, he told me, very neat. When he got the call, he would take his shopping bag with the tools, and I'd make him a sandwich to take along, and off he'd go. Come home after I was asleep, but very quiet and considerate, he was."

It was too late to go to Westbury, even if we knew where to go. As we left, I gave her a fifty, told her to buy some flowers for his grave. I had a feeling she would spend the whole fifty on flowers, plus a few dollars of her own, which was not what I intended. They don't make them like that anymore.

On the street, walking back to my car, I asked Warren, "Notice anything?"

"By its absence, Dad. No drafting table, no drafting instruments, no tracing paper. Also no typewriter and no typing paper."

"Freehand sketches, Slowicki said, but you still need a pad and a pencil. And a sharpener. Typing can be done, if it isn't too much, in a store. But it's more likely that the machine shops, where he worked nights, was where he typed his notes and made his sketches. Poor old people learn very quickly how to save pennies."

"You're probably right, Dad, but we should still check it out tomorrow morning. I'll let you know when I've found the right places."

VIII

"But I thought we weren't allowed to give you advice," Iris Guralnik said. She had come to the limited partners' meeting without her husband because Marvin had a headache. She said. I knew better. Marvin never got headaches; he gave them.

"You're allowed to give all the advice you want," I told them. "It's not illegal. But the moment you do, you take on all the responsibilities and potential liabilities of the general partner. And you don't get paid for it."

"That's what I meant," Iris said. "So why did you call us all together?"

"The way I work, I want you all to know what's going on. Although right now it looks like Kassel's murder won't hurt us much, you never know. One way could be if the tests show some problems, we won't have the benefit of Kassel's knowledge to help us fix things. We may be filing an inferior embodiment of the speaker."

"Can't Borovic open the box and see what's inside?" Jerry Fein asked.

"Sure he can," I said, "when he gets it, but maybe Kassel gimmicked it so that if you open it the wrong way you wreck something or change something. I don't know. He was a suspicious old nut. Then there's always the possibility that Borovic may not understand what's inside.

Slowicki, the patent lawyer, said the speaker worked on a completely new principle."

"Isn't Borovic supposed to be a genius speaker designer?" Bob Pasternak asked.

"Yeah," Iris said. "That's why the HHF-2 was last year's big flop. Ten years ago he was a genius. Today? Who knows?"

"Gentlemen," I said firmly, "and Iris. You're getting awfully close to giving me advice. My decision is to wait, which we have to do anyway; the police won't let anyone into the dead room for at least another few days. Slowicki says it will be filed in a week, so first we're going to look at the application, then, when Borovic is sure he knows what's what, he can open the speaker enclosure. One other thing I'm thinking: Maybe Kassel keeps one important screw or resistor or something in his pocket and sticks it into the speaker at the last second. Without it, the speaker self-destructs. So I want to know exactly what was in Kassel's pockets before I let the tests continue and I'm going to tell Hamilton that tomorrow, first thing. And I'll call Slowicki to ask the police for the contents of Kassel's pockets."

"So what do you want us to do?" asked Len Vogel.

"Give me ideas on the murder. That kind of advice you're allowed to give, and that's what I need badly."

"You're trying to solve a murder case?" Iris looked incredulous.

"Why not?" I shot back. "You think the police are smarter than we are? In normal cases, yes, but this is a real weird case. They'll never solve it in a million years. We've got lots of high-powered brains right here in this room."

"What do we care if the murderer is caught or not?" Dan Tumin asked.

"Because one of our executives did it," I said. "And they all know it; they're not stupid. The company will fall apart if each one of them is busy being suspicious of everyone else instead of attending to his job."

"I'm inclined to agree with you," Irv Waxman said. "I'm not in criminal law, but it's pretty clear it wasn't a crime of passion and it wasn't a mugging for his pocket money and it wasn't an accident. It was a well-planned and well-executed crime in a place and at a time when no outsiders were around and no lower-level employee could get to Kassel easily or had a motive. But I don't see a motive for any of the top executives, either. Do you?"

"Frankly, no," I admitted. "But give us a chance. You've forgotten it's only one day, not even."

"Us?" Iris asked.

"Warren and me. He's been very helpful." I almost added "surprisingly."

"All the executives make a little extra money with Kassel dead," Len Vogel pointed out.

"Peanuts," Monroe Baum answered. "All the money we agreed to pay Kassel goes into the estate escrow account anyway. All we save, and we benefit along with the executives, is Kassel's consulting fees for the first year. Five percent of that is not enough inducement for a man to risk jail for. Or even twenty-five percent, in the case of Carter Hamilton."

"Sex?" Iris asked. "Are any of the boys that way?"

"If they are," I replied, "I don't think a seventy-year-old machinist is a prime-type sex object to kill over."

"Maybe he's an SS man, hiding out. He did have a slight accent, you said." Dan Tumin's idea. "Maybe Borovic has relatives in Yugoslavia or someplace like that."

"We'll find out after the autopsy," I said, "if he has a blood type tattooed in his armpit. But then, why not kill him in Mineola, where he lived? Why in the plant where suspicion would fall on one of a small group? Any other bright ideas?"

"Blackmail?" Jerry Fein asked.

"For a hermit who never went anywhere and got practically no mail or phone calls, Jerry? Not unless he had ESP."

"Was there any relationship between Kassel and any of our executives?" Iris asked. "It may not seem like big money to you, Al, but you projected that he would be getting at least a hundred thousand a year, four years from now. Maybe one of the execs is Kassel's illegitimate son or something and wanted to get the inheritance before Kassel changed his will."

"Slowicki doesn't think Kassel had any relatives at all, but even if what you say is true, why kill him now? Why not wait until the speaker is working perfectly? In fact, why take the risk at all? The old man was seventy and a smoker. Be patient a few years, get Kassel to recognize the relationship, and you inherit anyway."

There were no other ideas. As we started to break up, Iris came up to me. "Tell Warren to take your car home. I'll buy you a cup of coffee and drive you home later."

At last I would find out why Marv Guralnik had a sudden headache at exactly the time of the meeting.

IX

"How did you get away?" I asked Iris as we settled down to our coffee and Danish. "I thought you saw patients at night."

"Clients, Ed, not patients. Psychiatrists have patients, psychologists have clients. I just canceled out, usual female excuse, said I had a headache."

"Why did you take me to this Howard Johnson's?" I asked. "There are two others much nearer."

"It's the only one in Nassau with a motel attached," Iris grinned. "You want me to lose my reputation as a sexpot?"

"I hadn't thought of that, Iris," I said, "but you're right. If one of our local gossips saw you having a midnight snack with a man just to talk business, they might even go so far as to tell your husband."

"It isn't business, Ed. I want to talk about Warren."

"My Warren?" This was so unexpected I couldn't even think of a wisecrack.

"You know any other Warrens, Ed?" She hesitated for a moment and took a sip of coffee. Her Danish was still untouched, so I knew she was serious. "You're going to ruin him if you keep doing what you're doing."

"Me? Ruin Warren? You're crazy, Iris. I'm doing everything I can to make him a man."

"Exactly. You know, Ed, if you came to my office and

paid for it, you'd listen to me carefully. So make believe this is costing you fifty dollars an hour and I'll tell you a big secret, one I would normally have told you only after twenty weeks of consultation and analysis and preparation. Feel flattered, Ed, that I trust your maturity and good sense to spring it on you cold."

"So tell already. Stop with the heavy buildup."

She looked me straight in the eye and said, slowly, "Warren is not you."

"This is the big secret, Iris? Would you believe I already know that?"

"You know, but you don't know. Let me put it another way. Warren is different from you. He will never be another you, no matter how hard you try to make him you. But if you push him hard enough, you can make him be not Warren. Then he won't be anyone."

"Is that what you're getting at? I assure you, Iris, I am not pushing him to copy me. Everything he wants to do, I let him. Even help him."

"So tell me, Ed, why does a twenty-five-year-old man have to be let do anything?"

"Because he's not a man, yet, I'm sorry to say."

"What's a man, Ed?"

Not an easy question; I had to think for a while. "In this case, Iris, someone who can take responsibility for himself and others."

"This he's not doing?"

"He still lives at home, Iris. With me."

"Why, Ed? He can't afford an apartment?"

"Of course he can, Nassau Venture Capital pays all its employees a living wage. Even relatives."

"So why is he still living with you?"

Usually I don't think about things, I just know. Iris was making me think, and not by needling me either, the way she usually did. "He loves me," I said. "That's the only thing I can come up with."

"He couldn't love you if he had an apartment in Great Neck or Roslyn?"

Iris was good at her work; no argument. It was just that I had never seen this side of her before. She waited. I thought. Finally, I had to say it. "He feels responsible for me. Wants to help me."

She nodded, satisfied. "I came to the same conclusion, Ed. So by your definition, he's a man. And he's highly intelligent. How's his book coming?" She didn't try to rub it in, just changed the subject.

"All right, I guess. He reads me parts, but I can't understand it. The technical jargon I could learn, I suppose, if I put my mind to it, but epistemology? The whole concept has to fail. How can you know how you know what you know? It's circular, goes nowhere."

She hesitated, and studied me carefully, her Danish still untouched, her coffee cup still almost full. "I didn't intend to get into this, Ed, but we might as well. Does everything you do have to succeed?"

"No. I've failed before, but there has to be a *chance* it will succeed."

"Why?"

"If you can't gain anything by trying, no matter what, why start trying? You're a top golfer, Iris. Would you set your goal at going around eighteen holes in seventeen strokes?"

"That's different; Ed, mathematically impossible. But trying to understand the process of understanding is not impossible, it's just *almost* impossible. So you tell me, Ed, why should anyone try doing it, or worse, devote a lifetime to trying?"

I hate thinking. This kind, I mean. Analysis of a design, or a financial statement, or a corporate structure, that's one thing. But with abstract thinking, I don't have to think, I know. In spite of my not having a degree, I have a very quick, accurate mind, ask anyone. I know the answer while everyone else is still trying to understand the problem. But with Iris leaning forward, staring at me as though her life depended on it, or my life even, I had to think abstractly. It wasn't easy.

Finally, I put it all together. "There are four reasons to work on epistemology, or anything like it," I said. "One, you have to try. Or you feel you have to try. Human beings are not made to give up. If you don't try with all your might, you'll go through life feeling terrible, frustrated. You'll feel dead all your life."

"Good." She nodded approvingly.

"Second, even if the odds are a million to one against, you might succeed. And if you win against those odds, :hat has to be the greatest feeling in the world."

"Every human being alive today, Ed, is the successful conclusion of a struggle against odds much greater than a million to one or a billion billion to one. That's another good reason to cherish, to protect human life." She leaned back, pleased.

I continued. "I never looked at it that way before, Iris, but you have a point. Then there's the information you can pass along to others, even if you fail. To say, 'I've tried this road; no go, it's a dead end.' She gave me a look. "All right, Iris," I conceded, "I'll try to be precise. You can transmit to other investigators the information you have gotten, and your analysis and your conclusions, so that they can use what you did and failed at, to help their investigations. Like an inheritance."

"You're beginning to think like a philosopher." She smiled encouragingly.

"And last, your work, your investigations, even if you don't succeed, if you just carry knowledge a little further along, you're helping humanity, everything."

"Wrong, Ed. Try again."

"I'm wrong? No I'm not." I thought about it. "If you . . . Oh, I see what you mean. Increased knowledge doesn't necessarily benefit humanity; it depends what you do with it. If the politicians get hold of it, if they know how we know things, they could manipulate people better, like slaves. But that's only in the short run. In the long run, humanity has to benefit from learning."

"That's an interesting idea, though there are people who would dispute that. They feel that exploration should be channeled and controlled. Why don't you discuss this some evening with Warren?" She had a satisfied cat smile.

"So that's the whole idea? Okay, Iris, I will, but what makes you think Warren will want to discuss things like that with his uneducated old father? I don't even have a bachelor's and his IQ is thirty points higher. He thinks I'm stupid."

"Just try it, Ed, you might be surprised. It might even end up with his getting his own apartment."

"That's all I have to do? Just talk to him?"

"Not just talk. Discuss ideas, feelings, how you see things. Let him feel he can open up to you. When he finally does that, then you know you've succeeded."

"I talk to him plenty. About everything. What is in my heart is on my tongue. You know that, Iris. Especially you."

"You talk *at* people, Ed, not *to* them. And you hardly ever listen. Discuss means two ways, not one imposing his views on another."

"I do that?"

"Not necessarily intentionally, Ed, but you do come on strong. You're a little above average in height—and in weight, too, Ed, start thinking of your health—but when you walk into a room, it's like an army came in. You act ten feet tall, dominant, and in your own way, domineering. And your voice—when you talk to someone, it's like you're shooting cannons at him. Even with Warren. This does not make for intimacy. Or openness."

"It's hard to talk to Warren, Iris. He's got a very fresh mouth. Every chance he gets, he sticks in the needle."

"And you don't? Where to you think he learned it from?"

"Even so, a son should respect his father."

"What do you want, Ed? A man or a mouse?"

This took some digesting, and the coffee was cold, so I ordered some fresh, hot coffee. "Eat your Danish, Iris. It's okay, I'll do it. Thanks for the therapy. Someday, maybe, I can return the favor."

"Don't talk like the evening's over, Ed. That was part one: the test. I wanted to see how flexible you were, if you were as quick as I thought. You passed, did beautifully. Now I want you to keep your mind open a little longer."

"First you tell me I'm running my own son. Then you want me to practice philosophy. Finally, I'm a bully. And last, it's not finally. What else do you have to make me feel great?"

She looked at me appraisingly, then took the plunge. "There's another place where you shouldn't interfere with Warren's life."

I looked at her, puzzled.

"I want you to stop pushing Warren to date Judy Fein," she said.

"Why, Iris? Judy's a nice girl."

"Judy's a terrific girl, Ed. She'd make some guy a great wife if he were smart enough to realize it."

"So what's wrong if I hint a little to Warren? And how do you know about what I tell Warren?"

"You don't hint a little, Ed, you give orders. And a soft voice you don't have, that's how I found out. It's bad for Warren and it cheapens Judy. She needs all the help she can get; a raving beauty she isn't."

I was beginning to get the picture. "You wouldn't have somebody in mind for Warren, would you, Iris?"

"Just keep your hands off, Ed," she said, warningly. "Let nature take its course."

"They hardly know each other, Iris."

"They had two dates before Lee went back to school. She thinks he's very nice."

"Lee could easily win the Miss Universe contest, Iris. You don't have to fix her up."

"I'm not fixing her up. I just don't want *you* screwing things up."

"If you're in a hurry to get Lee married off, send her to work in New York. For General Motors. In one month she'll be Mrs. President of General Motors. Just don't send her to Washington; we can't afford the President taking his mind off foreign affairs right now."

"I don't want her to make the society pages, Ed, I just want her to be happy. And I'm not in a hurry to marry her off; that can wait until after she graduates. I just want her to get engaged."

"And you think marrying Warren would make her happy? If she really wants him, all she has to do is give him one look. The right kind. He's so inexperienced he'd fall over backward right away."

"Sure, provided you don't talk against her. Warren respects your judgment."

I was trying to be polite. "Lee isn't exactly an intellectual giant, Iris."

"I know. A B average is considered very respectable in most places, but in our circle it's the kiss of death. But that's really unimportant; Warren is smart enough for both of them. The husband and wife don't have to be equal in everything. In fact, it's better if they're not. Look at my marriage, Ed, and yours. You were very happy, weren't you?"

She was right. In spite of the difference between me and Thelma, I couldn't think of any way my marriage could have been better. Except if it was longer, of course. "I see what you mean, Iris. I was very proud that Thelma had all those degrees and was smarter than I was."

She looked at me peculiarly. "Yes," she said, "I guess she was. And it's even better when the husband is smarter. So what do you say, Ed? Are you going to keep your big hands off?"

"I wasn't trying to force him, Iris. But maybe you're right. Okay. I'll stop pushing Judy. But I won't push Lee, either."

"Fair enough, Ed. But keep two things in mind: one, Lee loves children, wants a big family, and two, if Warren is going to be a success, he needs a wife like Lee. She's a perfect hostess, poised, friendly, and memorably beautiful."

"In the venture capital business, Iris, what he needs is the ability to see the potential and the pitfalls of a business."

She looked at me in exasperation. "Don't you listen, Ed? He's not going to be in the venture capital business, and certainly not with *you,* meaning *under* you. He's going to be an academic or an author or a consultant, whatever comes about. The one place he shouldn't be is in your business, especially since you're so good at it. Unless . . ." She stopped and thought.

"Eat your Danish." I reminded her that I was still here.

"What you were talking about tonight, Ed," she mused. "That may be just the way."

"My problems with Hamilcar? That will be the way? To what?"

"Not Hamilcar, you'll take care of that; you're good with business problems. I mean the murder."

"The murder will be just the way? Iris, speak English."

"What suddenly struck me," she said, "was how Warren could get the confidence he needs, to learn that he can make a positive contribution on his own. That his training has value. That way is to solve the Kassel murder."

"Warren?"

"You said he was helpful to you. This is a crazy kind of murder, the way you described it. The police are never going to solve this case, you can be sure of that. You won't, either, with your pragmatic businessman's approach. Only Warren can."

"But Warren knows absolutely nothing about real life."

"He's smart; he'll learn fast. But you mustn't stop him or discourage him."

"Me?" I was insulted.

"Who else? Remember what we discussed before? Help him and encourage him, Ed. Swallow your pride, hold back on your bulling ahead."

"You want me to throw the game, Iris? I never in my life did that. I always played to win."

"Not throw the game, Ed. Just hold back a little. Let Warren win, for once. You can come in a close second."

I shook my head. "If he finds out, he'll never talk to me again."

"So don't let him find out. Be subtle." She smiled wickedly. "Besides, he may beat you to it anyway."

"You should live so long, Iris. But okay, I'll give it a try. What do you say I should do?"

"Let him take the lead; you act like his assistant. Be a Watson to his Sherlock."

"I never thought of Warren as a detective."

"He's solved tougher problems than this in his thesis. Give it a try, Ed, it might just be what your son needs: to succeed on his own where his father couldn't. To solve an insoluble problem, to save his father's business, and to bring a criminal to justice, all at the same time. It would make a man of him in his own eyes."

"And in mine, too, Iris. Okay, I'll do it, but it won't be easy; I'm too used to leading."

"Don't worry, Ed, I'll be around to remind you when you slip."

I sighed. "That's what I was afraid of. Eat your Danish, Iris, you have to keep your strength up." At least I had the last word.

X

I could understand why Democritos Thanatopoulos, owner of Precision Products, Inc., of Westbury, New York, didn't want to talk to us. For all he knew, we were agents of the Department of Labor or the IRS, and were wired. But I had to know what he knew about Walter Kassel.

Warren broke the impasse. "Mr. Thanatopoulos, if we wanted to make trouble, all we'd have to do is phone some government agencies. Kassel's landlady gave us your name and location; she could give it to others. If they started investigating your little business, you might have problems."

Finally, the heavyset, dark-eyed young man spoke. "I didn't do anything. The government wants to check my books, go ahead."

"What would happen if the government put a man with a movie camera at your door every night?" Thanatopoulos glowered at Warren. "I have some questions about a hypothetical machine shop," Warren said. "Call it Alpha. Maybe you can help me, Mr. Thanatopoulos."

"You talking about a company that don't exist, right?"

"Exactly. This is a small company, only a limited space and a limited number of machines. The boss makes a living, but he can't afford to get a bigger place or more machines or to pay more workers. Sometimes there isn't enough work coming in for even his few steady employees, and he has to send them home early, with short paychecks. But if he does this too often, they're going to go elsewhere, right?"

"That's the problem with all the small business. Everybody knows that."

"But sometimes Alpha gets a big order, a rush. He can't handle it, but if he turns it down, the customer goes elsewhere and maybe never comes back."

"You say no to a good customer, better to close up the shop quick."

"If you give part of the work to another shop, you lose, not only the profit, but you take the responsibility for bad workmanship and lateness, plus the cost of double handling."

"Why should Alpha help his competitors and lose money, too?" Thanatopoulos looked at Warren as though he were a fool.

"On the other hand, Alpha can't afford to put his workers on overtime. Not only won't they produce well when they're tired, but he'd have to pay them time-and-a-half."

"In this business," Thanatopoulos said, "you could lose a job for one cent a part. Small guys can't afford overtime."

"So the sensible thing is to bring in a night shift. But who?"

"Should not be union," said Thanatopoulos, entering the game. "Should not be somebody who is already tired from a full day's work."

"There are some old men, good workers, retired, who are willing to put in a night's work now and then. Men who are trustworthy, won't talk because they don't tell Social Security their income."

"Men like that, they treat machines with respect; never forget the oil and they hold tolerance good. No mistakes."

"And if Alpha pays them in cash, he can pay piecework,

so he knows what his production costs are, exactly." Warren had really picked up a lot in the few months he was with me.

"If he pays cash, Mister, he pays below scale, because of no taxes. Everybody wins. And no records." He smiled at Warren triumphantly.

"But what happens if someone gets hurt? Doesn't Workman's Comp investigate?"

"No Workman's Comp, Mister. The old men, they're too smart to get hurt. That's how they live to be old. Also, the old men are independent contractors. They sign a paper to hold harmless. Alpha keeps papers in a safe place, not in the factory."

"Don't these old men want to make something for themselves?"

"Sure, all the time. Old machinist, he always makes things. Bad to stop them. Cannot stop them, unless the boss, Alpha, is here all night."

"As long as they finish their work, Alpha doesn't care what they do?"

"Wrong, Mister. Alpha always must care. Old men can only use scrap. If he must use new stock, leave note what he takes. Deduct from pay, but only at cost. Also, if he dulls tool, he must sharpen himself. No charge for electricity."

"You do only metalworking here, Mr. Thanatopoulos? No wood?"

"Different business. Different machines, different tools."

"Thank you, Mr. Thanatopoulos," Warren said. "It's been very instructive talking to you. One last thing. Do you have a partner or someone who helps you in your business?"

"No partner, no helper, no relative. Not enough here for two families."

Driving back to the plant, I remember what Iris had told

me, and congratulated Warren for the way he got the information from Thanatopoulos.

"Thanatopoulos was easy, Dad, compared to Aristotle,
Plato, and Zeno. Are you going to give whatever we've
found out to the police?"

I was about to say yes, when I realized that this was the
perfect time to start shifting control of the investigation. "I
don't know, Warren. What do you want to do?"

He didn't have to think. "I'd like to give the police
everything we know or have heard. They'd appreciate the
cooperation and it may help them find the murderer
quicker. This would unseal the anechoic chamber sooner.
But I wouldn't give them our analysis, and especially not
any conjecture. They might feel we're trying to interfere
with their work or even beat them to the solution. That
would make them uncooperative."

Clear thinking, Warren. Keep up the good work, and I
could end up with six beautiful grandchildren a lot sooner
than I had thought possible.

XI

Little Rollie Franklin was not his usually cheerful, dapper self. His gray hair was mussed, and the collar of his navy blue silk shirt was open. His desk was loaded with piles of advertising layouts and computer printouts. The walls of his office were covered with blown-up magazine ads for Hamilcar speakers, like a teenager's *Star Wars* posters. Speaker displays stood in every corner. For Rollie, every day was a super-saleathon, and his office was the battlefield.

"How am I expected," Rollie asked the ceiling, "to prepare a sales campaign for a super-breakthrough speaker, when I don't even know what the production model is going to look like? No photography, not even a drawing. I got to go to the distributors and retailers handcuffed."

"Can't you fake it?" I asked.

"These days?" He looked disgusted. "Everybody's an expert these days, even ten-year-old kids. Each one subscribes to three testing magazines and every one of them knows more about intermodulation distortion than I do. No more 'full rich sound' or 'covers the full range of audibility.' Now they want curves of tests I can't even pronounce."

"Would it kill us to hold off another month or two?"

"Kill us?" He pulled at his slim black moustache. "It will bury us. The Las Vegas Winter Consumer Electronics

Show is in six weeks. You want me to go there with a handmade, tweaked-up model that every critic will ask what's wrong with the production model? And even if I have to do that, what do I tell everybody? That I can't take orders? That I *can* take orders but I can't give a delivery date? That sonofabitch has been dragging his tests out for three months already, would you believe it? Three whole goddamn months?"

"Are you saying you want to skip the winter show, Rollie?"

"Did I say that, Ed?" He looked at Warren for confirmation. "Did you hear me say that? You think I want everybody in the trade laughing at me? Do you want to drop a million more into Hamilcar? What do you need a sales manager for, Ed, if you got nothing to sell? I'll make a living, a good salesman can always make a living. There's a terrific corner near Penn Station where I can buy a spot for a hot-dog wagon, but what about Carter? He's not fit to be anything but a president."

Just then the intercom buzzed. "I'm in conference," Rollie said. "Hold all calls."

"It's your mother's nurse," his secretary's voice came through.

Rollie muttered an excuse and picked up the phone, his usually animated face stiff. I made a motion to leave him in privacy, but he waved me back. Finally he spoke. "I don't care what he says, if she doesn't want to go, she doesn't go." He listened for a bit longer, then spoke again, decisively. "Then do it. Three shifts, seven days." He hung up, looking tired, his face gray. His eyes seemed unfocused, looking at . . . I don't know what.

I waited for a few seconds, then spoke. "I know a lot of people, Rollie, at the community hospital. They were my wife's friends. It's a good hospital, one of the best. Maybe . . ."

"She wants to be at home." He was still looking straight ahead. "With me."

"I know what this can cost, Rollie, and I know what you make. And . . ." I hesitated. There was no nice way to put it, but I had to say it so I could get to the important part. "And I know what you have. I had you all checked out, you know." He didn't move a muscle. I cleared my throat. "I'd like to lend you . . . interest free, of course . . . you can pay me back after the Kassel hits."

"Thanks, Ed," he said. He was still avoiding my eyes, but this time deliberately. "It'll be better if I go to a bank."

I respected that, and I understood, but I was investigating a murder, so I would have to come back to it. But later. Right now was not the proper time to follow up on that line, so I said, "The Kassel speaker is really good, Rollie, isn't it? Won't it sell no matter when we introduce it?"

"Sure, but how many?" he replied. "You think everybody is taking a vacation? You think I don't know what's going on in the trade? There's rumors Cleebin has a terrific new box, half the price of our 1A. And Dolman has a new woofer that will make the floor shake. And Golstyne's new electrostatic from England? It's supposed to wipe all the American speakers off the map. People are going to buy those, they'll all get good ratings for sure. So what happens when the Kassel finally comes out? 'Sorry, Rollie, the market's saturated. Everybody's already bought all the speakers they need. Call us next year, Rollie.' I'll die."

"What do you want to do, Rollie?"

He looked at me mistrustfully. "You really want to help, Ed?" I nodded. "Good. I've been thinking. We'll do it right now. You get John to meet us at the airlock. Warren tells the cop at the door that there's someone trying to kill Russo down at the other end of the plant, and runs there with him. I run in, grab the speaker, and pass it to John. When the cop gets back, he doesn't even know the speaker is missing. Meanwhile, you get Waxman on the phone to get Warren out on bail. What do you say, Ed?"

"Why don't you pull the cop away yourself, Rollie?" I asked politely.

"I'm needed here; Warren isn't. Just in case he doesn't get out on bail, I mean."

"Warren is a weak-willed young man," I pointed out. "If the police put pressure on him, he'll squeal. Turn you in. Then the speaker may be ready on time, but who'll run the sales campaign with you in jail?"

His face fell. "Yeah. Well, it was an idea. You got anything better in mind?"

"Sure. Warren is investigating the killing." Warren looked surprised at this, but he kept his mouth shut. "If you'll answer some questions, Rollie, you'll help solve the murder, the police will leave, and we'll get back to normal again."

"Shoot," he said. "What do you want to know?"

Warren moved his chair to face Rollie directly. "Who among the executives didn't like Mr. Kassel?"

Rollie's whole attitude changed. He was no longer the jolly, jumpy, fast-talking sales manager. With the typical salesman's ability to take on the coloration of his customer, he became the serious senior executive of a troubled corporation. "Do you really believe one of us did it, Warren?"

"There is no doubt of it, Mr. Franklin. Did you have anything against Mr. Kassel?" I admired Warren's subtle shift in person. I didn't know if he did it deliberately or instinctively, but it was exactly the right way to go. Iris was right. As usual. The kind of complex analysis this case needed was right up Warren's alley, and his soft way stood a better chance of succeeding than my tougher approach.

"We all disliked him, Warren. He was nasty, suspicious—completely unwilling to do things in the normal way. And he was slow. I don't mean a little bit, I mean a lot. He cost us time and money, really cost us."

"Did you ever discuss this with him?"

"Had it out with him a month ago. Pointed out that I was the one who gave him his break and now he was giving me the shaft."

"What was his response?"

"He wouldn't look me in the eye. Just said that he had to make absolutely sure everything was perfect before he would release the speaker for production."

"You accepted that?"

"I told him if he kept screwing around long enough his stock would be worthless when he got it. You know what he said? He had the nerve to tell me that maybe he should show his speaker to another company."

"He couldn't do that legally. Didn't you tell him?"

"Sure I told him, but I don't think he was listening or gave a damn for contracts."

"Did you really mean that, about going bankrupt if he didn't speed up the testing?"

"I wasn't kidding about missing the Consumer Electronics Show. The time to hit the market is when you've got the product. Who knows which genius is going to come up with an even better speaker next year? Licensing to Japan could have made us a million, cold. You, too, Warren, not just us. He cost you plenty, remember that."

"Yes, but my father and I weren't in the building at the time; the six of you were. And you all know your way around the anechoic chamber."

"We didn't do it, Warren, none of us. I'll admit I was glad he was killed; I figured it would solve my time problem. It didn't, I'm sorry to say, but I didn't think far enough ahead at the time."

"If you had, you would have killed him some other place? You hated him that much?"

"Come on, Warren, I never said we hated him. We disliked him. You don't kill a guy for *dislike*."

This was my opportunity to get back on the track, to pressure Rollie a little. "True, Rollie, you don't kill a guy for dislike. But maybe there were other reasons. Tell me, Rollie, why didn't you ever get married?"

"How could I ask . . . ? What girl would . . . ? There were lots of reasons, Ed. Lots."

"You wouldn't let anyone hurt your mother, Rollie, would you?"

"Nobody, Ed. No way." He looked straight at me. "What's on your mind, Ed? Say it."

"Kassel was killing your mother, Rollie." I hoped I was saying it gently.

"Kassel didn't even know my mother existed, Ed." He grew tense. "What are you getting at?"

"Kassel was killing your ability to take care of your mother, Rollie, by taking so long to do the testing."

He kept silent for a moment, then spoke, controlled, tight. "If Kassel, or even you, Ed, tried, just tried, to hurt my mother directly, he'd be dead, Ed. Right that moment, he'd be dead. But Kassel wasn't trying to hurt my mother, or even me. I can't figure out, no reason, why he was screwing around, but it wasn't to hurt me, that I'm sure of. Or my mother."

"But it *did* hurt you, Rollie. And your mother."

"If Hamilcar goes under, I'll get a job selling. Maybe I'll have to hold down two jobs, but I'll survive. And so will my mother."

"But that won't leave you much time to be with your mother, Rollie, will it? Nowhere near as much as if Hamilcar was successful."

Rollie Franklin just stared at me. No answer was really needed. We both knew.

Warren broke the impasse. "Are there really millions riding on a production model of the speaker getting to the show on time?"

Franklin looked at Warren, then at me. He addressed Warren, his voice flat. "That's my projection, and I'm a pro."

"What projection?" I broke in. "I never saw your projection, Rollie, all I saw was Sambur's figures, and he never talked in those numbers."

"George is too smart for his own good," Rollie said. "He felt that if he showed you my projection you'd be scared off."

"Damned right I would, Rollie, unless you could back it up. Which you can't; you don't know what's in the box. Or do you?"

"I don't have to know all the details, Ed. I know it's smaller than the HHF-1A and quite a bit lighter. That's enough."

"I thought Kassel never let the speaker out of his hands. How did you weigh it?"

"Kassel weighed it for me. The first time he demonstrated his speaker, I had two HHF-1As on each channel of my setup. He had to unhook the speakers on one side to connect up his speaker. He really struggled to lift each of the 1As, but put his speaker in place easily."

"Are you telling me speakers are priced by the pound?"

"Not quite, but right now I'll guarantee that the Kassel won't cost any more to produce than the 1A, and will probably come in for a lot less. Ask Russo if you don't believe me. What do you think they make drivers and crossovers out of? Gold? Hell, we all use copper, aluminum, and iron, ceramic magnets, wood enclosures. We all work to the same precision."

"And what will the sales price be, Rollie? What Sambur projected?"

"No," he said firmly. "I'm going to put it out at fifty percent more than the 1As."

I was really surprised. "I was satisfied with the ten percent Sambur projected. Are you sure? Won't that cut us out of a big chunk of the market?"

"I'm the only one here who ever sold retail, Ed. I know. If I can get a production model to the winter show I'll have every retailer who hears it creaming. I might even cut the discount a point or two, if it goes good. How do you like that?"

"If you're right, Rollie," I said, "if you're right, our net will triple this year alone. You're talking big money, Rollie. Isn't that a motive for killing Kassel?"

"I'm the dumb one here, Ed, the only guy without technical training, the guy who doesn't think like an engineer, thank God. I'm sure that all the others know that with Kassel murdered we couldn't get into the chamber. So if any one of us killed Kassel to speed up production, we wouldn't kill him in the chamber."

"By your own logic, Mr. Franklin," Warren said, "you're the only one who thought Kassel's death could get you to the show on time."

"I know I didn't kill him and you should know it, too. It took a good technician to know how to do it; I'm just a lousy salesman."

"It seems to me, Mr. Franklin, that you're a lot smarter than you let people see. Anyone could have the flash of inspiration to show him how to commit murder in that place. If an uneducated machinist like Mr. Kassel could invent the greatest speaker of the day, certainly a brilliant sales manager could figure out a simple way to kill an old man in the anechoic chamber."

"I'm stupid, Warren. Tell me how I did it."

"I don't know yet, Mr. Franklin. But when I find out, I'll tell you guys second, right after I tell the police."

"There's another thing you should consider, Warren," Franklin said, very quietly. "Producing and selling a new product, with our time limitations, will take the combined effort and total, I mean absolutely total, commitment of every member of the Hamilcar team. Taking one man out of the picture, even if he's a killer, will ruin everything. Hamilcar could go under and your father and his friends could take a big beating."

"That makes an interesting ethical problem, Mr. Franklin. What do you suggest I do?"

"Drop it, Warren. Leave it to the police. Put all your efforts into getting the police to unseal the chamber."

Warren looked at me searchingly. I kept my face absolutely still. This was his decision, maybe his future. Warren turned back to Rollie Franklin. "Where were you at the time Kassel was killed, Mr. Franklin?"

"That's your decision, Warren?" Rollie's manner turned hard and cold. "Okay. I don't have to cooperate with you. You want to know anything, ask the cops."

Warren didn't flinch. "Mr. Franklin, I will soon have a half-interest in Nassau Venture Capital, and I'll be a stockholder in Hamilcar Hi-Fi. Now that Mr. Kassel is dead, I will be on the board of directors. I am asking you these questions in what I feel is the best interests of the company."

"What will you do if I don't answer?"

"Figure out what you would do if you were in my place," Warren said quietly. "Now double it."

Franklin looked as though he were sizing Warren up. Whatever he saw, and don't forget, half of Warren's genes are mine, Franklin folded. "I was walking back and forth," he said, "near the airlock. Not so often that I would really be noticed—I didn't want the employees to see how nervous I was—but enough."

"Did you see anyone?"

"The other executives? Sure. Most of them, at one time or another. Only Carter wasn't around. Playing it cool, I guess."

"Were the others near the airlock?"

"More or less. I kept moving and so did they. Every once in a while, our paths would cross."

"Did you see anyone hanging around near the airlock door?"

"No, we were all walking. Sometimes one or another would cross near the door. I did, too."

"Did you see anyone go in? Or come out? Or touch the doorknob?"

"No."

"Would you tell me if you did?"

"Not you and not the police. And I hope the others, if anyone saw anything, would have sense enough not to, either."

"You would protect a killer?"

"Kassel was over seventy and not a very nice guy, either. My whole life is at stake with this company. How many jobs you think are out there for forty-year-old sales managers of audio companies, huh? Especially for sales managers of companies where sales didn't go too good the last two years? So, if you want to put one of my people, who I can't live without, in jail, fine. Do it. But do it next year, after the new speaker is established; I'll even help you then. But not now. And if you want to quote me at the next board of directors meeting, go ahead. I'll make it easy for you, I'll repeat what I just said: that I'm putting the company ahead of everything else. So you think it over too, Warren, and maybe you should talk to your father and the other limited partners. And now, if you'll excuse me, I got some worrying to do."

In the corridor Warren turned to me. "Kassel was . . ." he said hesitantly, "in effect, he was killing Rollie's mother, wasn't he? The way you said? By his slow testing, Kassel was making Rollie miss the Las Vegas show, so the company would go broke and Rollie wouldn't have the money to keep his mother at home."

"I was just pushing him, Warren. I don't really know if that was the case. But," I said cautiously, "I can see how Rollie could take it that way."

"What do you think, Dad? Did I do right, threatening him that way?"

I answered fast this time, because I was getting the hang of it. "If I told you to lay off, would you?"

He didn't have to think, either. "No. I'm sorry. I respect your judgment, but I have to do what I think is right."

"I'll back any decision you make, Warren, whatever it is." I remembered what Iris had told me. "Even if I think you're wrong, I'm with you. But you can't go wrong if you do what's right."

He glowed. I hadn't realized how tense he was. It was flattering, in a way, too, that he wanted me to approve what he would do.

It would be nice, I dreamed, to have Warren really like me. And to have a beautiful, old-fashioned daughter-in-law and six beautiful grandchildren.

Now all Warren had to do was solve an impossible crime. Fast.

XII

We found our controller, George Sambur, in the lunch-room. It wasn't really a lunchroom, just an area on the lower level with benches, tables, and vending machines; a place to eat the lunch you brought from home when it was raining, or to grab a coffee-and when you wanted a break from the office.

George was having a hot chocolate with two chocolate doughnuts, just what he didn't need with his figure, but I guess he had to have something to lift his spirits these days. Since he was the youngest of the executives, he used chocolate instead of Scotch, thank God. Through thick glasses, his sharp black eyes showed he was not too happy to see us. "I get tired of looking at numbers all day," he explained guiltily. "Have to give my eyes a change of scenery."

"Yes," I said, "red numbers will do that every time. But black numbers, I never get tired of seeing them."

"We'll be in the black when the new speaker hits the market, Mr. Baer."

"If it ever does, George. Right now, Rollie says we'll never make the Winter Consumer Electronics Show."

"I can authorize enough overtime to make up the delay, Mr. Baer."

"Overtime costs money, George."

"I'm not sure it would have happened any sooner if

73

Kassel had not been killed. He was taking ten times as long testing as John. Even if we lose a day or two now because of the police, we'll make it up when John takes over."

"Why do you think Kassel was taking so long?"

"At first I thought it was because he was an amateur, being so fussy and secretive. But then it became clear to me that he was doing it deliberately, just to get the consulting fee for that much longer."

"You really think anyone would delay making big money just to get four hundred bucks a week for a few extra weeks?"

"You're looking at it from your own point of view, Mr. Baer. Look at it from his. When you're living on four hundred a month, four hundred a week looks very tempting. His contract called for one year's consultation after the filing of the patent application, but no limit to the time *before* filing. He was trying to delay the filing for as long as possible, pure and simple. He was killing the company for a few thousand dollars. I should have realized it and put a limit on the prefiling payments, but it never occurred to me that anyone could be that stupid and small-minded."

"How did you handle the situation, George?"

"I did what I always do. A week ago I presented my findings to Kassel and asked him to explain the facts."

"What was his explanation?"

"Nothing. He told me that he could take as long as he wanted to test the speaker, just like that. And he laughed in my face."

"And you did nothing?"

"What could I do? He was right. I had no control over him."

"That doesn't sound like you, George. You've never backed down for anyone when you thought you were right, not even me."

George remained silent, staring at his chocolate. I probed gently. "Did you tell Carter what you had found?"

"Carter would have . . . gone crazy if he found out."

"So you kept quiet," I knew I was on to something, "just to protect Kassel from being killed by Carter?"

He glared at me. "Or was it," now I knew for sure, "to protect yourself from being killed by Carter?"

He nodded wearily, not looking up.

"What did Kassel threaten you with, George?" I asked gently. "That he would now take an extra week to file the patent application?"

"Month," George bit the word off.

The way he said it, I smelled something. So I probed. "What does that 'would' mean, George? That if you bothered him again he would take a month or more? Or that, since you accused him, he was *now* going to delay another month?"

Sambur stared at his hot chocolate. The icing on his doughnut was melting in his fingers.

"Another month would have killed the company," I said softly, "wouldn't it, George? You might even miss the *Chicago* show, right? What did your projections say about that, George?"

He looked up at me like a condemned man. "The company would have gone under, Mr. Baer. Even your investment wouldn't have helped."

"You were right, George," I said, "Carter would have killed you for just doing your job well. And killed Kassel, too. So you killed Kassel first? Clever, George. Very clever."

"I didn't, Mr. Baer. But I'll authorize a raise to whoever did."

"So it was a benefit to us that he was killed?"

"If you put it that way, yes. Wait until John takes over. You'll see how fast we'll move."

"You called Kassel an amateur before. Is that the right name for the inventor of a great new speaker?"

"It certainly is, Mr. Baer. He may have had that flash of

genius one time in his life, but that's it. I'll bet he couldn't design a simple bass-reflex speaker if you put the handbook in front of him. And he certainly couldn't make the proper decisions as to which speaker characteristics to emphasize at the expense of which others. These are things that John and Carter do automatically, that any professional does, every day."

"Is that why nobody here is crying over Kassel's murder?"

He had the grace to blush. "None of us actually wanted him killed, but I'll bet we all . . . I know that I did . . . hoped that, at his age, in the natural course of events . . ."

"But one of you decided to hurry things along. Why, George?"

"I didn't say anyone from Hamilcar did it. All I said was that it helped the company that he died when he did. If one of us did it, why didn't he do it two weeks ago instead of so near the deadline?"

"What deadline, George?"

"I didn't mean deadline," he flustered. "I meant the date of the Las Vegas show. It's coming closer every day. You benefit, too, Mr. Baer, more than any of us. Why are you accusing us?"

"I'm not accusing anyone yet. And it's true I benefit equally with you guys, but there's one important difference. My whole life doesn't depend on Hamilcar; yours does."

"We're all young enough to start over again."

"Rollie Franklin? Come on. And can you see Carter working for somebody else? Or starting a new firm? Can you see John Borovic, designer of the flop HHF-2, being hired by anyone in the business? And you? Who wants a controller who let his firm go bust? Let? Caused, I should say. Directly."

"I could go into business myself. I'm ready."

"After you declare personal bankruptcy? There are very

few idiots in the loan departments of banks. No, George, you'd have to start at the bottom again, as a bookkeeper in a supermarket. You each had a motive, a strong motive, to kill Kassel."

He stared at me coldly through his thick glasses. "Motive isn't enough, Mr. Baer. I'm angry with you right now and you're angry with me, but neither of us is killing the other."

"There are different levels of anger, George. What I said is nothing compared to the real problems you guys face. Start over, you said? With what? From where? Maybe the others don't realize it, but you sure as hell do. You six are personally, repeat personally, responsible for all the debts of the company, now. All, George, not just my four hundred grand. That means if Hamilcar goes under, you have no home, no car, no nothing. If that isn't a motive, six motives, I don't know what is. So don't give me any bull about you guys not having enough incentive to kill Kassel."

He folded. What other choice did he have? "Very well, Mr. Baer. I see your point. How can I help?"

"That's better," I said. "Start by telling me where you were when Kassel was killed."

"I don't know when he was killed, exactly, but from after lunch until two I was wandering around the plant, checking that the records and time sheets were up to date."

"Did you see any of the other executives?"

"All of them, on both levels, except Carter. But that doesn't mean anything. It's a big plant with lots of corners."

"How do you think Kassel was killed? You have a logical mind, how *could* it have been done?"

"Would you believe, Mr. Baer, it couldn't be done? I've been puzzling over it, purely as an intellectual exercise, since it happened. It don't know all the details, but from what I gathered, there was no possible way for Kassel to have been murdered."

That I didn't need him to tell me. I turned to Warren. "Anything else you want to ask him, Warren?" Warren shook his head. I decided to leave Sambur with something to worry about. "I'm sending Monroe Baum over tomorrow to check the books," I said coldly, "just in case some changes have been taking place in the last few days."

He didn't twitch a muscle. "You can check my books anytime, Mr. Baer, without notice; it's your prerogative. But you don't have to say it in an insulting manner. And if you bother to think about it, you'll see that there is no way Kassel's death could help me if I were cooking the books. And just to shake you up a bit in return, I'm good enough with numbers and computers so that if I wanted to embezzle funds, it would take you and Baum a year to find it out, and another year to figure out how." He gulped down the rest of his cold hot chocolate and stalked out on his short, stubby legs.

XIII

I got refills on our coffee and Danish so Warren and I could talk. The lunch break was over and the lunchroom practically empty, so we didn't have to whisper. "So how do you like our executives?" I asked. "Potential killers, eh, every baby-faced one of them?"

"You should really be happy. They would do anything to keep the company going."

"That's not always good. A human being should have limits. Would you kill to save your business?"

"I've discussed things like that many times. It's one of the simpler problems of ethics. God said, 'Thou shalt not kill.' Under no conditions? Obviously not. So what are the conditions under which *you* would kill? To save the life of your wife? I know the answer to that one. Your children? Me? I think you would. I hope I am never faced with that problem but, if I am, I hope I am able to do what is right, even kill, if that's what I should do. It boils down to a weighing of values."

"But you're still going to find Kassel's killer, aren't you?" He didn't know what was at stake here, I'm sure. For him, I mean.

"I have to find the killer, Dad. Not just because it's right, but because it's an intriguing problem, one I can't resist."

"For the pleasure of solving it?"

"For the same reason you're trying to break a hundred, Dad. Because it's there."

"Okay, I get the point. So what do you think of our fat little friend, George Sambur?"

"He's a possible. But I can't believe that any one of these guys would kill someone just to get the speaker to the show on time."

I hated to say it, but it had to be said. "You've never been poor, Warren. You don't know how terrible it can be or what the thought can do to a man."

He looked at me sympathetically. "Don't feel bad that you always made a living and I missed the experience of starving as a kid. But if you think I wasn't aware of the hard times, if you think I didn't know when you and Mom sat up nights figuring out how to meet the payroll or how to stay in business another week, then you didn't know me. Kids know these things, no matter how hard parents try to hide them."

"We weren't trying to keep things from you. We just didn't want you to worry unnecessarily."

"I know. I wasn't criticizing you. I just wanted you to know I understand. My problem is that I don't see the Las Vegas show as important enough to kill over. The Chicago show, or even the New York show, would accomplish almost the same thing."

"You think there's another motive?"

"There has to be. But what?"

"Well, Carter Hamilton wants to steal the Kassel speaker. Not only for the money, but for his ego. He wants people to respect him."

"I agree with that," Warren said, "and I'd like to add that he also wants the speaker named after him. That seems to be very important to him."

I nodded. "The clothes he wears, that shows he's very interested in what people think of him. But is that enough motive for murder?"

"Maybe it's not 'people'. Maybe it's one person."

"The only person . . . His girl friend? Betsy?"

Warren shook his head slightly, started to say something, then stopped. I waited. Still nothing. So finally I had to ask. "Why not his girl friend? Who else is there?" Warren sipped his coffee, carefully not meeting my eyes. Then it hit me. "His father?" Warren sort of shrugged a little, still looking away. "But his father's dead. How can he satisfy his . . . ?" Warren just looked at me. "He can't, can he, Warren? Is that what you mean? That no matter what he does, he can never . . . ? Then it *really* hit me, what Warren was telling me. And I couldn't talk. Not now. What could I say? "I love you, Warren?" Right now? Five minutes ago I could have said it, should have said it. Now was just the wrong time. "I'm proud of you, Warren? Most of the time? Even if you're a philosopher?" If I had said it before, years before . . . But what's done is done, and what's not done . . . I *would* say it. Soon. Out loud. At the right time. When it wouldn't look deliberate. But all I could say now was, "Maybe you're right, Warren. Let's talk to Gorman. He and Carter roomed together at school, so Fred has to know how Carter felt about his father."

Warren went along with my sidestepping. "While we're at it, we shouldn't neglect Gorman as a suspect."

"Definitely not. He's still on the list. Something he said is bothering me, but what, I don't remember. The trouble is, I have a bulldog mind. When I'm digging, concentrating on one line of thought, I can miss something right under my nose."

"That happens to everybody, Dad, not just you. It'll come back, let's get back to Fred Gorman. He's a lot smarter than Carter, and much more devious."

"That's for sure. But I don't see him risking a murder charge so he can be president of Hamilcar. His way would be a lot more sneaky."

"Framing Carter for murder is sneaky enough for Iago."

"Yeah, but Iago didn't do the killing himself. You think Fred might have found a way to con Carter into killing Kassel?" I thought for a moment. "Nah, too complicated. Also, there's no evidence against Carter. If he was framed, there would have to be some evidence by now."

"Well, Carter is pretty intelligent himself. Maybe he figured out a foolproof way to kill Kassel. What we have to look out for now is Fred's planting a clue to implicate Carter."

"If it's intelligence you're after, George Sambur is the boy genius around here. And he had a terrific motive: Kassel was, in effect, blackmailing Sambur, forcing him to keep his mouth shut about the extra month Kassel was going to take to complete the tests. That way, the company would have gone under and Sambur would have been to blame. Yet Sambur couldn't do anything about it. Other than to kill Kassel, that is."

"The knowledge of that motive died with Kassel. If George hadn't told us about it, no one would ever have known."

"I pinned him down; that's when he told us. He had to tell, just in case someone had overheard. If he had concealed it and was found out, it would point to him as the killer. By telling us about it, he looked innocent."

"That could lead to an endless cycle of who thinks who knows what. What about Rollie Franklin? He's nearer your generation than mine."

"Rollie is a man in a bind, a very big bind. He's chained to his mother, given up his life for her, that's clear. Also, he's over forty, which in this business is the kiss of death. And he needs money desperately. So he's got all the motives you want. But he's no technician, and this murder had to have been done by an expert."

"Rollie impresses me as being very shrewd, Dad."

"Sure, but there are plenty of shrewd guys who don't know how to screw in a light bulb."

"Do we know that tricky technology was involved?

Maybe Kassel was killed in some simple way that we just don't see."

"I'm not counting Rollie out yet; I just don't see him as the killer."

"Because he's good to his mother? Because he's Jewish? Or because you take pity on him?"

"All of these, if you want to know. But mostly feel. I pity the other guys, too, but I'll face the facts if we ever find out who did it. Let's find Borovic or Russo, maybe we'll learn something from them."

When I was a kid, we had a game, If. If we had ham, we could have ham and eggs, if we had eggs. Each kid, in turn, tried to keep it going as long as possible. One we never used was, If we had the motive, we would have the killer, if we had the method.

XIV

John Borovic's door was open and his secretary was away from her desk, so we walked right into his office. It was more an engineer's drafting room than an office, with handbooks and catalogues scattered over all the horizontal surfaces. The wall opposite the door was covered with framed citations, awards, and blown-up reviews of the HHF-1 and 1A. I noticed there were no reviews of the HHF-2.

John had his huge feet up on his desk, leaning back in his swivel chair, hands behind his head, eyes closed. "This is how a great designer works," he said, without opening his eyes, "so no wisecracks about my easy life. Who is it?"

"Your partner, Ed Baer," I said, "and if you're dreaming up a super-duper design, tell me to go away."

"I wasn't designing anything," he said, taking his feet off the desk. "Just trying to figure out how to get the speaker out of the anechoic chamber without getting arrested."

"You can't wait another day?"

"Another day, okay," he said, "but suppose it's another week? Or more? You've got to use your influence, Ed. You know a lot of politicians."

"Sure I do, John, but every time I talk to a politician, it costs. Why the rush? I can understand why we have to get to the Vegas show, but Slowicki will have the patent application filed in a few days anyway, and then we'll know what's in the box."

"It's not the same, Ed. Patent papers give only general information, not specifics. It's the little details that make the difference between a good speaker and a great speaker." Borovic stood up and began pacing nervously. Although no taller than Fred Gorman, he was at least fifty pounds heavier, built more like a linebacker than an engineer. "I have to know what Kassel did, exactly, to get such good results."

"Can't you tell from the test readings you have so far?" Warren asked.

"What I can tell doesn't make sense." John pushed his straight black hair off his forehead. "Normal frequency response curves have peaks and dips all over the place."

"And the curves for the Kassel don't?"

"You'd better call it the HHF-10 or Carter will have a hemorrhage." He smiled for a second. "No, the HHF-10's curve is practically a straight line."

"That's good, isn't it?" Warren asked.

"Oh, sure," John said sarcastically. "So is perpetual motion. I used to dream about such things. Here," he reached into his lower drawer and threw a mottled black-and-white student's bound notebook on the desk. "Here. Every designer has one. Every time you have an idea, no matter how crazy, you write it in the book and sign and date it. Just in case it should be workable." He riffled the pages in front of me. "See? Hundreds of dreams, wild guesses, designs. You know how many of them are worth anything? One, that's how many. The one that became the HHF-1A. I keep another book like this on my night table at home, for when I wake up from a nightmare with an idea. So if some layman has figured out how to make a speaker with a perfect top, middle, and bottom, I want to see what's inside."

"Did you ever talk to him? Ask him for a hint about the design?"

"Once. He turned very nasty, accused me of trying to steal his speaker, and of being jealous of his genius. Said if I bothered him again he'd have me fired, can you imagine? I was ready to slug him."

"You *were* a bit jealous, weren't you, John?"

"It's sort of humiliating that a creep like that can come up with something better than us pros."

"Jealousy can be a powerful motive, John."

"Come on, Ed, we're all jealous of one another in this field. You think the others don't wish they had come up with the 1A? I'm jealous of Cleebin, Cleebin is jealous of Dolman, Dolman is jealous of me. And we're all jealous of Golstyne; he brings a new miracle out of London every four years. So what?"

He was too sure of himself, so I stuck in the needle. "Was Golstyne jealous of the HHF-2, John?"

For a moment I thought he was going to slug *me*, so I shifted in my chair to free my left foot for a knee kick. Then he slowly and carefully straightened out the plastic photocube on his desk with the pictures of his wife and their four little girls. I wished that we, Thelma and I, had had a little girl, too, the way we had once hoped, one that looked like Thelma. Not for remembering, I didn't need that, but just because it would have been nice.

Touching the pictures seemed to calm Bovoric down, but he still spoke in a very measured way. "The 2 was a very competent design. It did exactly what it was supposed to do. You think everybody has golden ears? Or likes to hear real music? Hell, most of the people out there have never, and I mean never, heard live music. The so-called concerts they go to are all amplified and distorted. You can even buy commercial distorters in case your guitar doesn't sound dirty enough. They want a boomy bass and a metallic treble. That's what we were shooting for and that's what we gave them. If the market hadn't shifted we'd have sold a million of them."

"But you didn't, and the fact remains that you were not only jealous, you were dying of curiosity to see what was inside the enclosure."

"I was anxious to get to work on improving the design."

"I thought it was a perfect speaker."

"Nothing's perfect, Ed. If this mechanic had a once-in-a-lifetime idea, God bless him. But I guarantee I can make it better. I don't care how good it is now, when I finish tweaking it, it'll be perfect. He didn't know enough to do it. I do."

"You want the winter show model to be perfect?"

He looked at me as though I were an idiot. "Of course. All the critics will be there. And the other designers. But what I really want is that the production model be *almost* perfect."

"So Kassel's slow action frustrated you? Angered you?"

"Are you kidding? If any one of us had caught him alone, no witnesses, we would gladly have strangled him."

"Or knifed him?"

John stopped his pacing and stared at me. "You're serious, aren't you?" he asked. "I was just talking. Rhetorically, you know. You really think one of us did it?"

"John," I said solemnly, "don't take this wrong, but yes, one of you guys did it."

"You're crazy, Ed. Why? Sure we were all upset and frustrated, who wouldn't be, but you don't kill a guy for that. And what did it help? We still don't have the speaker. And why in the chamber? I mean, why in the plant at all?"

"Don't you have any ideas?"

"No. He had to have been killed for some reason that had nothing to do with the speaker. If it did, why in the dead room, of all places? He used to take the speaker with him wherever he went, even to the toilet. He took it home at night in a shopping bag, like an old lady. Can you grasp that? A million-dollar speaker in a paper shopping bag? I used to worry that the bag would tear and the speaker fall out and break or get lost or something. So if the speaker was it, why not follow him home, bang him on the head, and take the speaker? What's to stop you?"

"I don't know, John. It may seem stupid, but I feel it in my bones. His murder, where he was murdered, and how he was murdered, it all connects to the speaker."

"You're wrong, Ed. If someone wanted to steal the speaker, there were a hundred easier ways to get it. Just grab it out of his hands in the street and take off. He was an old man, any kid could have outrun him. You didn't have to take the risk of killing him."

"What good would having the speaker do, John? The patent application would have been filed in a week or two. How could anyone gain from stealing the speaker?"

"Lots of ways. Another company, any good engineer, could take it apart and figure out how to change it sufficiently so he could file for his own patent. It might not be granted, but it could delay things enough so that, for the next few years, no one would have a clear patent. Meanwhile, the other company could be pumping out speakers as fast as us."

"You're saying that Kassel's murder wasn't connected to the speaker?"

"Maybe it was, maybe it wasn't, I don't know. But he sure wasn't killed to get the speaker. After all, the killer didn't get the speaker, did he? It had to be something personal, not the speaker."

"If that was it, why do it in the dead room?"

"You got me, Ed. My God, talk about doing it the hard way, that's like doing it standing up in a hammock."

"I know, I know," I said. "That's another puzzle. You've been in the chamber lots of times. How is it to walk on?"

"Not too bad, if you walk slowly and carefully. The

trick is to take one step at a time, slowly, and wait for the oscillations to damp out before you take the next step. You see, the netting is sort of loose, wherever you stand becomes the low point, so if you move slowly enough, you're always in a stable position. As soon as the police let us in, try it yourself, I'll coach you."

"What will you do when you get your hands on the speaker, John?"

"First I'll complete the tests. Then I'll put the speaker on a bench, with Carter and Tony watching, measure it, and slowly take it apart, taking pictures from every angle and at every operation, with a foot ruler attached, for scale, just in case it's been gimmicked. I'll have a tape recorder handy and describe every move I make down to the most trivial detail. Then I'll put it together again and test it again, to make sure I did everything right and understood what I was doing. If it's okay, I'll give it to Tony to take apart and duplicate every piece. We'll test the copies against the original, and if they're okay, we'll make a dozen units and start varying the parameters and testing them. Meanwhile, Tony and George will work up a cost analysis, Rollie will start the sales campaign, and in eight months we'll corner half the market. Sounds good?" He glowed.

"Sounds great. Can Warren and I be there, at the initial incision?"

"Sure, if you don't breathe too heavily."

"Now let's get back to business. Where were you when Kassel was killed?"

"Are you back to that again, Ed?" His glow faded at once. "After lunch I walked around downstairs for a while, then I walked around upstairs for a while, then I walked near Janie for a while, then I went back here to think for a while."

"A perfect alibi, I see."

"If I had known I'd need an alibi, I'd have gotten one."

"Did you see any of the execs near the anechoic chamber?"

"Of course I did, everybody but Carter. We were all concerned about the test results. Carter was, too, but he likes to play cool. I was sweating blood."

"Don't get upset, John, I have to ask. Did you check the prior art patents? Anything useful in them?"

"I regularly get a copy of any patent issued remotely relating to speakers. You think I didn't go through the pile"—he waved at a stack of papers on his filing cabinet—"and Carter, too, trying to find some way of not paying Kassel?"

"Nothing?"

"Absolutely nothing. Lots of improvements but no breakthroughs, and nothing that would do what the HHF-10 could do."

"One last question, John. Of all the Hamilcar people, who do you think is the most likely to have killed Kassel? In terms of personality, that is."

He laughed a short, nasty laugh. "Don't take this wrong, Ed," he mimicked me, "but you asked the question. The most likely one, in terms of personality, is Ed Baer."

He was right, I think. In terms of personality, that is. But this didn't get us any closer to finding the killer.

"One more, Warren," I said as we left. "Tony Russo, the production manager. Then we'll have questioned them all."

"If we get as little from him," Warren said, "as we did from the others, we'll still be nowhere."

"Sometimes you learn something you don't know is important until, when it fits in with everything else, it turns out to be the key piece of the puzzle."

"I know, Dad. It's just so frustrating. We've been checking for two days now and we don't know the motive or even how it was done."

"We do know who had the opportunity, though."

"Yeah, everybody. That really narrows it down."

We went downstairs to find Russo. In spite of my trying to keep Warren's spirits up, he looked very down. I thought I was doing good by letting him take the lead in finding the killer, depending on his super-intelligence to solve the puzzle. Two puzzles, actually, the how and the why. I thought it would be the boost to his ego that he needed, the way Iris thought.

Maybe it was time for me to take the lead again. That way, when we failed, I could take the blame. That's what a father is for, isn't it? I'd decide after we spoke to Russo. Maybe I should talk it over with Iris, too. Tonight. She might have some ideas. And if *I* failed, *she* could take the blame.

That's what a psychologist is for, isn't it?

XV

The glassed-in office had a big clock with a sweep second hand on the wall facing Tony Russo's desk. Below the clock hung a giant calendar covered with colored pins and big notes in bright red ink. Behind the desk were bookcases filled with manuals and catalogues. No paintings on the wall, just posters pushing productivity. I was glad we had Russo working for us, and I thanked God I didn't have to work for someone like him anymore.

No sooner were we seated than a short, heavyset man in denims burst in. Ignoring Warren and me, he slammed his palms on Anthony Russo's desk and yelled, "I've had it, Tony. You've got to get rid of Cuccio before he kills somebody. Today. Right now!"

Russo rubbed both broad hands over his bald head and stood up slowly. No taller than the other man, he looked twice as wide, and it clearly wasn't all fat. "First of all, Bud," he said, jabbing his finger into Bud's chest, "when the door is closed, you knock, especially if I got visitors. You want these gentlemen to think we're all bums down here? Second, Cuccio is the business agent's brother-in-law, which is why he's here in the first place, and you know it. You think we got troubles now? What do you think will happen if I fire him?"

"Then get him out of warehousing, Tony. Let Joey get a few gray hairs for a change."

"You crazy? I put Cuccio in assembly, we might as well close the doors. What did he do now?"

"Knocked out Bigley's two front teeth, that's all."

"You kidding?" Russo's sharp black eyes opened wide in amazement. "He's twice Cuccio's size."

"It wasn't a fight. In fact, lucky I was there. I got right between them and saved Cuccio's life, like a dope. I caught one on the jaw, see?" He turned his head; there was a big red bruise on his cheek.

"What happened?" Russo asked.

"Cuccio had to get some 1As for an order and the little jerk was carrying a hook-on ladder to the end of the aisle. Bigley was pushing a truck and walked past just in time to catch the end of the ladder, the hook end, in his mouth."

Russo's face got red and his neck swelled. "Do you mean to tell me Cuccio was carrying the ladder *horizontally*? Didn't I give strict orders they were to be carried vertically? *Only* vertically? Goddam it, they're light enough, ain't they?"

"You give orders, I give orders, what difference does that make to a moron? He did it, and it's going to cost me my best man for a day, plus Workman's Comp. Plus, if we're real lucky, an OSHA inspector walks in today. You got to help me, Tony. You got to."

"I can't put him anyplace else, Bud," Russo said resignedly. "The warehouse is the least dangerous place for him. You just got to live with it. I got to live with problems, too; it goes with the job."

"I'm not trying to interfere with your operations, Mr. Russo," Warren said. "But may I offer a suggestion?"

Russo looked at Warren, then at me. I kept a poker face. It was clear that Russo felt that advice from a still-wet-behind-the-ears kid who had never done a day's work in his life was not precisely what he needed at this particular moment. Russo, however, was a seasoned executive and he knew that I controlled fifty percent of Hamilcar's stock, so he said, "I would be very pleased to hear any practical, constructive suggestions." His tone clearly indicated that he did not really expect any practical, constructive suggestions.

"It sometimes helps to look at a problem backward," Warren said. "Mr. Cuccio, I take it, is accident prone," Warren said. "So it would make sense to put Mr. Cuccio in a position where it would be difficult for him to cause accidents and where he would, in fact, have to think of preventing accidents, and nothing but that."

"Such as?" Russo sounded skeptical.

"Why not put Mr. Cuccio in charge of OSHA compliance? Make him responsible for the occupational safety and health of the plant."

Russo looked dumfounded for a moment. Then he laughed. Probably the first laugh he'd had in weeks. "Perfect," he said. "Absolutely perfect. The dum-dum will have to concentrate on safety all day long, be an example to the others. He won't dare cause any accidents himself; how would it look? And we can tell the business agent it's a promotion."

Bud looked sour. "It ain't gonna work, nothing will work with that yo-yo. But if it gets him out of warehousing, I'm all for it. Thanks, Tony." He looked at Warren. "Thanks, kid, I owe you one."

"This is my son, Warren," I said. Proudly. Warren shook hands with Bud, who left rubbing his cheek, and with Tony Russo, who was starting to look harassed again.

"I'm sorry to bother you when you're this busy, Tony," I said, "but I have to ask you some questions about Kassel's murder."

"My job," Russo said. "I'm always this busy. You'd think a simple thing like a loudspeaker, two models is all we got and we're only making the 1A right now, you'd think they could make them blindfolded, wouldn't you? You want to have some fun? Spend a day with me here, any day. You wouldn't believe how they can screw things up. Every day I learn a new way."

"How did you get along with Kassel?" I asked.

"Marvelous," he said bitterly. "What did you expect? That dumb Dutchman wouldn't even let me touch the box. How am I supposed to set up a production line if I don't know what I'm doing? How big are the magnets? What shape? What material? Can I substitute off-the-shelf items, or is everything custom? What kind of crossovers, air core or iron core? Can I use standard drivers, or modified standards? Or what? New technology or can I use my existing machinery? You know when Rollie wants a *production* model? For the Vegas show! I can't even order cabinets and he wants a production model." Suddenly his face twisted in pain and he bent over, holding his big belly. With his left hand he reached into his vest and slipped a big white pill into his mouth. Slowly he straightened up and poured a glass of water from his desk carafe. He drank slowly, cursing between sips, "That bastard, that *stunad,* that miserable . . ."

"Kassel?" I asked foolishly.

"Who else?" he asked bitterly. "I'm not supposed to get excited, I have to stay calm. If my ulcer perforates again they may not be able . . . I'll have no stomach left. Only predigested food. You ever taste predigested food, Ed?"

"No," I answered, "but I can imagine."

"Kassel did it to me," he went on. "I'm glad he got killed, you know that, Ed? He deserved worse. You know why I'm glad, Ed? Because I would have done it tomorrow, otherwise. That was my limit, Ed, tomorrow. Then who would take care of my wife? My kids?"

"Take it easy, Tony." He wasn't doing himself any good this way, and I still had to talk to him about the murder.

"Take it easy? You kidding, Ed? I could take losing the company. We were undercapitalized, okay? We made a mistake on the HHF-2? Okay. I'm a man, I'll take my licking, no crying, no excuses. I'll go out and get a job. And I'll stay calm, my ulcer under control. But when a bastard like Kassel purposely . . . He was killing me, Ed. Purposely. When an ulcer gets to be a certain size, you can't stop it."

"I understand, Tony." I tried to calm him down. "We all understand your problems, Tony. I'm trying to help, but I need your help to get the police to let us take the speaker out of the anechoic chamber."

"Yeah, that's what Gorman told me. You're going to solve the murder. Do me a favor, Mr. Baer: Don't solve the murder. Just tell Sergeant Palmieri to let me have the speaker. As far as I'm concerned, killing Kassel was the best thing that could have happened, only it should've happened a month ago. I even thought of . . . you know what I did? I offered to let Kassel have Cuccio as a helper, that's the kind of risk I was willing to take."

"How was that a risk, Tony?"

"Maybe Cuccio breaks the speaker instead of Kassel's neck, huh? You think Cuccio ever does *anything* right?"

"So you wanted Kassel dead?"

"Don't give me that, Mr. Baer, I didn't kill him. Listen, in any one week I want everyone in this plant dead. Even Carter. Especially Carter, and he knows it; it goes with the territory. But do you see any bodies laying around? What I think and what I do, they're two different things."

"What did you do after lunch, Tony?"

"First of all, Mr. Baer, I don't eat lunch. Every hour or two I drop into the lunchroom and get a container of milk. Sometimes with a cheese Danish," he said, patting his waistline. "It gets pretty boring, plain milk. With my hiatus hernia plus my ulcer, I got to keep something down there all the time, otherwise I might not be able to smile once a day, just to show that I don't really hate everybody all the time. So I can't afford to eat lunch, otherwise I'd be fifty pounds over instead of twenty."

"Did you go upstairs at all about one o'clock?"

"Upstairs, downstairs, all over. You think you can run a plant sitting on your butt? Every day I got to see what new stupidity some yo-yo has figured out so I got something to think about at night when I can't sleep."

"Did you see anyone near the airlock?"

"Everybody but Carter. You think Gorman is too cool to sweat? Or Sambur? We're all in this damn swamp together, and the alligators are sharpening their teeth. We *need* that speaker, Ed, need it bad."

"You're an improviser, Tony, you figure things out good and fast. How do you think Kassel was killed?"

Russo's eyes dropped to the desk, and he began snapping a pair of ring magnets together. "I don't know, Ed. It doesn't figure." He looked ashamed at not knowing the answer. "I've been thinking about it, trying to figure it out, for two days. There's no way it could have been done. Unless there's somebody here who's a lot smarter than I am. Maybe a spring gun, like for scuba divers, to shoot the knife? Or a trapeze hanging from the top somehow? Real crazy things like that, that's how desperate I was. But it couldn't be, otherwise the cops would have said something."

"Maybe they're keeping things quiet," I said, "while they complete their investigations."

"Look, Ed, I'm an engineer. I know machinery and I know people. Production manager isn't just giving orders and checking reports, you know. I solve problems, I solve them every day, and I solve them in real time, fast, while the meter is ringing up dollars. Maybe once in a while a creep like Cuccio will stop me, but only for a day, that's all. If Warren hadn't come up with his idea, you think I wouldn't? But this killing, it's giving my ulcer an ulcer."

"You mean you didn't figure out yet how he was stabbed?"

"That's what I'm telling you, Ed. Only the killer knows, and don't look at me that way. If I was the killer, believe me, you'd never even find the body, and I'd be building the production line right now. Have you ever been in the chamber?"

"No, Tony, never even seen the inside."

"Let me tell you, it's bad enough just to walk in there. The net sags under your weight, you know. Kassel wasn't about to let anybody come in that room, you would have heard him scream over Janie's speaker a mile away. And there was no way you could step on that net without Kassel knowing; it's like a spider web. So if the killer sneaked in, even if nobody saw him sneaking in, Kassel would have said something."

"What if the killer was there ahead of him?"

"I thought of that, Ed, you think I didn't? So where was he standing that Kassel didn't see him? If he was all the way in the back, he'd still have to walk forward to reach Kassel, and then the old man would have yelled something. He had a big, loud mouth, you know. Besides, you think an exec can disappear for fifteen, twenty minutes and nobody notices? We're not IBM, you know, we only have us six, and we work."

"So you think an executive did it?"

"Sure. Who else? A worker leaves his machine, it goes on his foreman's card. He goes in the wrong part of the plant, he's noticed. It had to be an exec."

"Why not an outsider?" I asked.

"No outsiders were here that day. If you were an outsider and wanted to kill Kassel, would you do it in the chamber? There's no better place? Come on, Ed, give me some credit."

"Suppose the killer sat on the concrete beam?" Warren said suddenly. "The one that supports the test frame."

Russo looked disgusted. "So Kassel walks in with the lights and the speaker. He sees the killer sitting on the beam. 'Wait a minute, Mr. Smith,' Kassel says, 'until I bolt on the speaker, then you can stab me.' You think I'd miss anything that obvious?"

"All right," I said, "the how we'll find out somehow. Who did it, Tony? I *know* you figured that out."

His eyes dropped to the magnets he was playing with. No answer. He stood up. "I'll tell you what I told the cops, Ed, and that's it. I didn't see anyone go in or out of the anechoic chamber. I didn't see anyone kill Kassel. I didn't do it myself. I have no evidence as to who did it. I don't know why he was killed here. Everybody I know is glad he's dead, but glad is no crime. And my guess could be wrong, so I don't point a finger at anybody. That's it. I got work to do. You want to follow me around, you're welcome. Otherwise, good-bye."

"If it got out," I said softly, "that you know who the killer is, you'll be dead in one day, Tony. You're a lot easier to kill than Kassel was. You'd better tell me what you're thinking, spread it around; there's safety in numbers."

"Is that just conversation, Ed, or are you hinting?"

"Take it any way you want, Tony."

He stood up and looked me straight in the eye. "If I thought you'd do a thing like that, I'd quit right now. But I know you better, Ed, and you know me better. So I know that you're just trying to make me say something I don't want to say. Your threat is all bullshit. You can apologize later. Or follow me around now, take your choice. I got work to do."

We didn't follow him. I was sure, from his reaction, who he had in mind. It had to be Carter Hamilton. But there was nothing more than personality behind that guess. And possibly the jealousy of the guy who had worked himself up against a guy whose father had staked him.

Walking to the car, I asked Warren, "Did you catch how mad Borovic got when I mentioned the HHF-2? He's a lot more jealous of Kassel than he lets on."

"Obvious, Dad," he answered. "But you should be able to understand that. In temperament, Borovic is very much like you. You've never been jealous of other contractors, but how would you feel if some amateur built a perfect building right after you messed up a job?"

"I'd feel lousy," I admitted, "but I wouldn't kill the amateur. What good would that do?"

"Precisely. If you wouldn't kill out of jealousy, pride, why should Borovic?"

"His temper. Did you see how quickly he blew up at me?"

"I also saw how quickly he cooled down. This murder was not a crime of sudden passion; it had to be carefully planned. And if you think you're always so calm and cool, one of these days have a movie taken of yourself playing golf."

"That's different. It's socially acceptable to hit a golf ball hard. Healthy, in fact. Russo would be a lot better off if he played golf. Get rid of his frustrations."

"Or maybe give him more," Warren said. "Russo is the type that makes his own frustrations. Do you think it's an accident that Russo is working in the kind of job he has? Can you visualize him as a bookkeeper?"

"Sure. I can visualize fifty broken pens a day, ledgers torn in half, and chief accountants getting their heads bashed in."

"Has Russo ever punched out anyone in the plant?"

"Everyone stays out of his way when he's really mad, even Borovic, who's a head taller and probably outweighs Russo. But if you ask me, I don't think Russo would actually . . . That's why he has ulcers. Because he's always keeping everything bottled up, not letting it out."

"Could he have killed Kassel?"

"Oh, sure. He's a problem solver, and if he thought Kassel . . . He's used to finding quick, neat solutions. But *could* doesn't mean *did*."

"It seems to me that you think any one of the six could have done it."

"I *know* that one of them did it; I just don't have any evidence that points to which one. Or if I do, I don't know that I have it."

Warren was quiet on the drive home, looking like he was thinking. "I want to sit down with you after supper," he said, "and analyze what we found out in the last two days. If we organize the information, perhaps a pattern will emerge."

I agreed. I wanted to see if his backward way of thinking could produce something with this kind of puzzle. The way he figured out what to do on the spur of the moment with the business agent's brother-in-law was really good stuff. Maybe when I was ready to retire, not for a long time, you understand, but someday, Warren could take over NVC instead of writing books. Maybe I'd even read a book myself. On philosophy, I mean. What could it hurt?

XVI

After Violet, God bless her, had served us coffee, I told her
to go home early, I'd clean up the supper dishes. She was
worried I'd mess up her kitchen, but I swore that I wouldn't
touch anything but the dishwasher. Actually, all through
supper I was anxious to get started with Warren, analyzing
the Kassel murder, but I didn't want to upset Violet.

"The problem of how he was killed," I said, "is a lot
more difficult than I thought it would be."

"I know," he said, finishing his coffee. "I'm sure motive
is the key, but if we find the mechanism, that may lead to
the motive."

"The trouble is the murder is impossible. If we assume
that the killer entered after—"

"Let's not assume anything, Dad. Why don't we start
with the three possibilities: the killer came in before, with,
or after Kassel."

"Okay, but make that four: before, with, at the same
time as, and after."

"I stand corrected, Dad. The distinction may be important. You would have made a good student of philosophy,
the way your mind works."

"You really think so, Warren?" He nodded. "In spite of
my not having a degree?"

"Aristotle never had a degree, either. In fact, I was hop-
ing that, with your mind, if you looked into philosophy,

especially epistemology, we could have some interesting talks. With your fresh, really innocent, viewpoint, I might get some insights I could use in my book."

"Steal, Warren, steal, it's all in the family. But let's apply our two different approaches to the problem at hand. How was Kassel murdered?"

"Start with them going in together. I'd eliminate that. Aside from his passion for secrecy, Janie Zausmer, and probably some others, would have noticed something that unusual. The same goes for their going in at the same time."

"Not necessarily, Warren. What if the killer went in through the downstairs door at the same time Kassel went in through the upstairs door?"

"Accepted. But for the moment, let's confine ourselves to the entry of the killer through the upstairs door. That means—"

"One more thing," I interrupted. "Everybody says that there are only two entrances to the anechoic chamber. Shouldn't we check if there are more? I don't mean just the plans, I mean physically check the entire exterior. Not that contractors go out of their way to put things in that aren't on the plans, but mistakes *are* made."

"I'd put that aside as a sub-case, Dad. It's a theoretical possibility, but highly improbable. Tomorrow I'll put on old clothes and go over every square inch of the chamber walls. Right now, let's assume the killer entered after Kassel. When did he enter?"

"Immediately after Kassel finished bolting the speaker to the test frame. One minute later and Kassel would have been on his way out."

"You're assuming that Kassel fell where he was killed, Dad. Couldn't he have been killed, say, near the door and his body dragged back to the test rig?"

"Why? You kill him anyplace, I don't care where, why move him? What's the point? And you'd have to move the lights, too. Leaving them in there would ruin the test, so Kassel had to be carrying them out with him. Besides, on the rope net, you couldn't move him so easily. And his clothes would get wrinkled and pick up fibers from the hemp or something."

"How do we know they didn't? We better get the police test reports. Let's go talk to Palmieri tomorrow."

"I was going to suggest that myself. We really should tell him what we know, although he probably has it all, and ask him for whatever he knows. Which he may not give us, so we better be nice to him."

"I would do that anyway. Okay, I think what you say is reasonable. We'll assume that Kassel was killed where he fell. The killer came in after Kassel finished bolting the speaker to the test rig; I can't imagine the killer spending time to do it himself. The question then becomes, how did the killer get to Kassel?"

"He had to walk on the net with the snowshoes. It's too difficult to keep your balance with plain shoes, even if your feet are as big as John's. There were extra snowshoes in the airlock; everybody knew that."

"Agreed. Now, when no one is looking, he pops into the airlock. Once in, he can take his time. He puts on a pair of snowshoes and walks into the chamber. The inner door is already open and the bank of sound-absorbing cylinders is pushed in. The moment he steps on the netting, Kassel feels it. Does he do nothing? Say nothing? I don't believe it."

"From what we know of Kassel, the least he would do is yell for the killer to get the hell out. Everyone in the area would hear it on the loudspeaker. Or Janie would hear it on the headphones."

"What if Janie is in cahoots with the killer?"

"Theoretically possible, but very *im*possible. You met her, Warren. She's clean."

"Just wanted to cover every point. Okay, maybe the

killer said something to the old man that would allow him to approach Kassel. Such as, 'Here's a check for a million dollars.' "

"It would be heard on the mike if Kassel could hear it. But suppose the killer shut off Janie's speaker while she was away?"

"No good. He'd have to go to Janie's test bank twice— once to turn the speaker off and once to turn it back on. Too great a risk. I'll accept that he took two big risks, one going into the chamber, and one coming out. But two more? No, that increases the possibility of being seen unacceptably."

"Okay, how's this? He waits for Kassel, hides in the airlock. The inner door is closed. Both doors, the outer and the inner, are heavy, soundproof. He kills Kassel in the airlock and carries the body to the test rig, not drags. Kassel was old and skinny, a young man could do it. He bolts the speaker to the test rig to make it look like Kassel was killed there, and lets Kassel bleed over the netting there. Then he carries the lights over, too. He had plenty of time."

"That's even worse. First of all, he gets blood all over himself. Then, the airlock is only five feet square, and has the light tripod and snowshoes in it. The inner door and the outer door both open into the airlock. Where would the killer hide?"

"Behind the outer door as it opens in. As soon as Kassel comes in, the killer shuts the outer door, stabs Kassel, catches the speaker, it shouldn't break, and goes to work. And he wears a smock to catch the blood. Later he takes it off and rolls it up and burns it in his fireplace when he gets home."

"Come on, Dad." Warren looked disbelieving. "How does he open the inner door with a body on the floor? And push in the bank of cylinders?"

"He props Kassel up vertically against the wall."

"With a knife in his heart? What about the distribution of blood on Kassel's clothes? Does he carry Kassel in the dark or does he carry the light pole like a candle? How does he hook up the speaker? How does he get Kassel's fingerprints on the bolts and tools and the speaker? I can just see someone carrying a dead body with a knife in it over the netting, wearing snowshoes and bouncing all over the place. What for? Why not just leave him in the airlock? The whole thing doesn't make sense. Kassel was killed right where he was found, and it happened right after he hooked up the speaker."

"Okay, you've convinced me. But that raises a whole bunch of other questions. Janie said— You know, we're assuming a lot of things we should check: That Kassel's fingerprints are on the speaker and tools; that Kassel's feet, snowshoes, rather, were next to the test rig; that the light tripod was five feet to Kassel's left; that the distribution of blood on Kassel's smock was consistent with his falling down there and not being moved; the whole *schmeer*."

"That's why we're going to talk to Sergeant Palmieri tomorrow. Let's hope he'll be cooperative. Meanwhile, we've got Kassel about a foot from the test rig, which means that the front of his snowshoes, before he fell down, were right under the frame that holds the speaker. So he was killed immediately after he put the speaker on the rig. Why then and not before?"

"That's what I meant. Kassel's face had to be inches from the front of the speaker. Did the killer duck under the speaker and the beam holding the test rig, or did he reach around Kassel from behind and stab him?"

"I can't imagine Kassel allowing anyone to walk around him and get under the beam to stab him, so it must have been from behind."

"Not necessarily, Warren. Stand up; you're tall. I approach you from behind, like this, reach around you with my right hand . . . I see what you mean. I'd have to have arms like an ape to get the knife straight in. So it had to be done with the left hand. Which of our six are left-handed?"

"They're all right-handed, except Gorman, but anyone can use his left hand. The point is, why in front? You're behind the man, why reach around him with either hand? Suppose he moved? Suppose he knocked your hand away? So the question is, why not stab Kassel in the back?"

"Yes," I said, "and why then, and not before? More, how did the killer know exactly when to kill Kassel?"

We both stopped. There were too many questions to which there were really no answers. At least for now. I poured out more coffee for each of us. Maybe if I didn't sleep all night I'd think of something.

"Okay," I said, finally, "we have three problems. How did the killer know exactly when to stab Kassel? How did the killer get to Kassel without his knowing? And why didn't he stab Kassel in the back?"

"Let's look at it backward, Dad," Warren said slowly. "Let's assume that the killer did stab Kassel in the proper way, in the heart from in front, with his right hand. When Kassel felt the killer coming toward him on the netting, he turned around. By that time the killer was on top of him and stabbed him. Kassel fell, and as he fell, he turned around so he ended up on his back. Or as he fell, the killer guided him so he fell on his back. The force of his fall made the light tripod fall, in its natural position, on Kassel's left."

"How did the killer know when to leap toward Kassel? Why did he guide the body's fall? And why did he wait until the speaker was hooked up?"

"He guided the fall backward to confuse us. He waited until the speaker was hooked up securely so it wouldn't get damaged if it fell off the test rig. He knew when to dash forward because he was in the vestibule, watching Kassel, or rather, standing on the rails of the movable cylinder bank, sort of leaning out just enough."

"These are very weak explanations, Warren. The test rig is about twenty-five feet away from the inner door, or twenty feet from the back of the cylinder bank. It took at least five or ten seconds to cover that distance on the net, probably more. Why didn't Kassel yell?"

"The killer signaled, somehow, that Kassel should be quiet. Whispered just loud enough to catch Kassel's attention and put a finger to his lips. Waved a fan of hundred-dollar bills, maybe. I don't know. But at least we have a possible explanation of the known facts."

"I wouldn't want to bet much over a nickel on it, Warren. But this also covers the possibility that the killer went in before Kassel did. He could have closed the inner door, pushed the rack of sound-absorbing cylinders back into place, and stayed on the right side of the rack on the netting. When Kassel pushed the rack in, there was no way he could have seen the killer."

"True," Warren said, "but why didn't he just stay on the left side and kill Kassel as soon as he pushed the rack out? Dropping the speaker is no excuse; the netting would have cushioned the fall. I'm inclined to believe that, of all the scenarios, the most likely one is that the killer came in after Kassel did."

"How do you figure that?"

"Suppose Kassel was delayed? Remember what Russo said about an executive not being seen for twenty minutes? This alone would point at the killer. An unnecessary risk. If he could get in easily, and it seems any executive could have with a fair chance of not being seen, the sensible thing to do would be to wait until after he sees Kassel go in."

"Okay, I'll buy that, Warren. Now let's analyze the killer's getting in through the lower door. Here we have worse problems."

"In some ways it might be easier. It's not as hard to get into the airlock; fewer people around, dimmer lights."

"True, but there are no showshoes in the lower airlock."

"It shouldn't be a big trick to put a pair in there in advance. Even if they're bulky, it could have been done after hours. And no one would notice one pair fewer upstairs."

"But if you're seen, it's like signing a confession."

"If you're seen, you kill Kassel at a different place."

"That's if you know you've been seen. A hell of a risk. You can't put a pair of snowshoes under a smock."

"One at a time?"

"Doubles the risk of being seen. And it would be very difficult to throw away a perfect plan for a perfect murder. Ask any mystery writer. I think it would be better to forget the snowshoes and walk on the edges of the cylinders at their intersections."

"You'd need a light for that, Dad."

"So you use a light, only you shine it downward so the reflection would be minimized. Kassel, working with a bright light concentrated on the speaker, might not notice."

"And again he might, and this would make him very upset. There could be a reason for someone coming in upstairs while Kassel is working, but downstairs could only mean trouble. Kassel would scream loud and clear. And why go to all that extra trouble?"

"It's one way to approach Kassel without his feeling your footsteps on the netting. That might balance out the difficulty of stabbing him straight in the chest from fifteen feet down."

"Not a minor difficulty."

"How about throwing the knife?"

"Through the netting? Standing on cylinders?"

"I know, I know. But it *was* done; we can't ignore that."

"I think we're going about this from the wrong direction. We should look at the overall picture, not the details. Why was the killing done in the anechoic chamber, of all the crazy places to do it? That has to be the most important clue, that the killer selected that place and time."

"Maybe you're right, Warren. We'll talk about that to-morrow. Right now, my head is spinning. I'm not used to all this concentrated thinking. Instead of philosophy, you should have been a Talmud scholar."

"I am, Dad. Modern American version. Okay, you go to bed, I want to think a little more. If you get up before I do, make an appointment with Sergeant Palmieri."

It was quite a while before I fell asleep. I had a nightmare, dreamed that I had graduated from school and become a philosophy professor.

Never should have had that second cup of coffee.

XVII

"Are you telling me," Sergeant Palmieri growled, "that you're going to withhold information from the police unless I tell you what we know?" Ben Palmieri wasn't much taller than me, but he filled his office full, and it wasn't all fat.

"Not at all, Sergeant," Warren said, "I'm going to tell you everything I've learned and I hope you'll tell us whatever you're allowed to."

Palmieri leaned back in his chair. "That's more like it. I'm promising nothing. Start talking."

Warren gave him a remarkably organized report of all we had learned in the past two days. Although Palmieri had a pen ready in his hand, he didn't take a single note. When Warren had finished, he said, "I see that I haven't given you any new information, Sergeant."

"We're slow but we're thorough, Mr. Baer," Palmieri said, "and you got to Thanatopoulos before we did. But you put it together nicely, professionally."

"May I ask a few questions?" Warren said.

"Depends on what."

"What was the cause of Kassel's death?"

"Stab wound in the heart. Ordinary kitchen knife."

"Straight in?"

"A thrust, like with a sword. Not downward."

"Was death immediate?"

"Practically. He was over seventy."

"Any blood spattered about?"

"Seeped out. On his smock and soaked his clothes."

"Any blood on the rope net?"

"Some dropped on the ropes."

"Was it consistent with his position?"

"Did he flop around, you mean? The fibers in his smock indicate he bounced a little when he fell, but basically he lay where he was found. He wasn't killed someplace else and then brought here, if that's what you're asking. Lividity was consistent with his position."

"When was he killed, Sergeant?"

"A little after one, probably before one-twenty."

"Were there any fingerprints on the knife?"

"The perpetrator used cotton work gloves that he must have disposed of. Not found so far."

"You checked the rubbish containers?"

Palmieri looked pained. "We're pros, Baer. The perpetrator had at least a day to dispose of the gloves off the scene of the crime."

"Does that mean you checked the garbage of the suspects?"

Palmieri just looked at Warren.

Warren smiled. "Who do you think did it, Sergeant?"

Palmieri's attitude changed. "Here's where I stop, Mr. Baer. You tell me, who do you think?"

Warren spoke slowly, seeming to choose his words carefully. "I have no evidence, not even a cohesive theory, but it seems to me it had to be one of the executives of the company."

Palmieri gave a short smile. "You're one of the owners of the company, ain't you, Mr. Baer?" Warren nodded. "And if it turns out that one of the executives did it, that'll hurt the company?" Warren nodded again. Palmieri looked as though he had come to a conclusion. "Okay, Baer, I appreciate that you've been straight with me, so I'll be straight with you. I've been a cop for twenty years, and I have a feel for things, at least in my profession. It ain't for publication, but I think the same way you do. Only," he hesitated, clearly searching for a way to get the idea across without actually saying it, "only, in a complicated case like this, the success rate has been on the low side, in the past. It's not like when a wife finds the husband's been playing around, or the boss finds his partner's been stealing him blind. When we know who did it, and how, all we got to do is get the evidence for the D.A. Which we're pretty good at. And usually, at least in this county, we got a pretty good idea who the perpetrator is. Usually."

"Do you mind," Warren asked, "if my father and I keep looking into the case?"

"As long as you don't interfere with my work, go ahead. You'll find we already talked to everybody by now, including the whole crew that was around the chamber. But one thing, if you come up with anything, see me first."

Warren promised he would. I spoke. "How much longer are you going to keep the anechoic chamber sealed, Sergeant? We have a valuable speaker in there that we have to work on. Hamilcar's business depends on it."

"The tech guys are finished. I was going to take my men off at the end of today's shift. But if it's that important, I guess I could do it now."

"Wait," Warren said suddenly. "Keep the chamber sealed. Please. Just for another day or two."

"Are you crazy?" I shouted. "We have to get that speaker fast. Did you forget about the show?"

"I'm tying up three shifts of two men there, Mr. Baer," Palmieri said. "You better give me a good reason to spend the taxpayers' money."

"I have a strong feeling," Warren said slowly, "I'm almost certain, that Kassel's murder is connected with that speaker, that Kassel was killed so that the murderer could get his hands on our new speaker."

"You think," Palmieri said, "that if I keep the chamber closed for a couple of days more, that the killer will be so anxious to get his hands on that speaker that he'll make a mistake, try to get inside, show himself some way?"

"That's my hope, Sergeant."

Palmieri thought for a moment. "You know," he said, "I've got other places to put those men. But okay, two more days, that's all I can spare. I hope you're right. I've got to justify this to the lieutenant."

Troubled as I was, I didn't say anything until Warren slid behind the wheel of the car. "You know, Warren, if this gets around, all the execs will be raving mad at you, not to speak of our limited partners. And if one of the execs is the killer, and he already killed once to get his hands on that speaker, he may get mad at you personally."

"I know, Dad, but it had to be done."

"Do you know what Palmieri is doing right this minute?"

"I can guess. He's letting it slip out that he's keeping the anechoic chamber sealed indefinitely at my request. Then he'll have a plainclothes cop following me to see who shoots at me."

"Brave doesn't mean you have to be stupid. From now on, you don't go anywhere without me. Where are you driving us to now?"

"Mineola. I want to ask Mrs. Dolan a few more questions I thought of last night."

I looked back. There was no car following us. In the movies, a trailing car is always a bad sign, but right now, I would have felt a lot safer with one.

XVIII

"Why, no," Mrs. Dolan said, "I just handed him the sandwich and he put it into the shopping bag himself. He never
would let me touch the bag, like it had a king's treasure
inside."

"What about when you cleaned his room?" Warren
asked.

"He took the bag with him and sat in the parlor until I
was finished."

"You never saw what was in the bag?"

"Oh, sure I did, you couldn't miss it. It was big and
square, as big as the bag itself, all wrapped up in brown
paper."

This much we already knew. Dead end. Warren changed
his line of questioning. "Did the other man who called Mr.
Kassel, not Mr. Thanatopoulos, did he ever give his
name?"

"No, he just asked for Mr. Kassel. Very cold he was, too.
When I asked who should I say is calling, he just said Kassel
knew him. They don't like to talk too much on the phone,
these people. It's the government they're afraid of."

"What was his voice like, Mrs. Dolan."

"Plain. Very plain, not a gentleman's voice like yours is,
sir, educated and all. No accent like Mr. Tinopolis."

"How many times did he call Mr. Kassel? The second
man, I mean."

"Every week, in the last six months. On a Monday, it always was. The first six months, about twice a month."

"When was the last time he called Mr. Kassel?"

"About a month ago, it was, I'm sure. I think Mr. Kassel got tired of working because this time he didn't go to work when he got the call."

"It was a particularly busy time?"

"Oh, yes. He had gone to Mr. Tinopolis three times that week already. Getting on in years, he was. But still a good worker, I'm sure. Otherwise, why would they keep asking for him?"

"Would you recognize the second man's voice?"

"I think I might, though my hearing's not what it used to be when I was a girl. I had a good ear then."

She insisted on making us tea, and brought out the tin of Danish butter cookies. Who's counting, but I noticed that there was the same amount left as when we had been there before. These were her guest cookies, I could see, but I ate one so as not to offend her.

Warren wanted to check out a few things with Lou Slowicki, so we drove to the shopping center where he had his office. Again nobody followed us. Either I was wrong about Palmieri's technique, or else he didn't have time to get a tail organized yet. Not that I believed either was possible, but the only other thing was that he actually *wanted* Warren to get shot. That kind of crime Palmieri could solve.

I kept checking behind us.

XIX

Lou Slowicki was just opening his office door when we got there.

"Do you always get to the office this late, Lou?" I asked, half joshing.

"Sometimes later," he replied seriously. "I'm trying to slow down. At my age, I'm entitled to take it easy."

"So why don't you just close up shop?"

"It's not that easy for a patent attorney. Some patents take three or four years. More. I can't leave my old clients in the lurch."

We talked in his office while he leafed through the mail. "Was Walter Kassel an old client?" Warren asked.

"No. He was my first client in over a year, and I'm sorry I accepted him."

"Why did you, Mr. Slowicki?"

Slowicki put the mail down and answered Warren patiently. "Inventors are a funny breed. Most of them invent for the pleasure of it. More than that, they can't help inventing. It's like an obsession, to obtain a patent on their brainchild. Very much like mother love, I'd say, and the patent is the only recognition they ever get. Most inventions don't make any money, either, and I'll explain that, but that doesn't stop them. They all feel that their particular invention will revolutionize industry, make them millionaires, bring instant fame, and save the world, typical

116

dreams we all have when we're young. And they're all young, inventors are, psychologically, full of hope, full of dreams. The amateurs don't want to know about, hear about, manufacturing, marketing, advertising, all of the necessary things to get a return on the invention, or even to break even on the costs of the patenting process. So when an old man, a man my age, comes to me . . . Kassel was a poor man, living on Social Security, with a dream, probably been thinking of this for years, what could I do? Throw him out? I took a ten-dollar retainer from him, any less and he would have doubted my sincerity, and looked at his sketches and descriptions."

"Did you really feel the device was workable?" Warren asked.

"The sketches were beautifully made. Kassel was a master machinist, and the descriptions were quite complete. Of course, the principle and the device were overdescribed, a common failing even among engineers, and the language was not perfect patent-application jargon, but I could fix that. He had obviously worked on this for months, patiently describing every possible embodiment. I thought, subject to what a search of the prior art turned up, he had a good chance of obtaining a patent."

"When did you order the search?"

"At once. I told him that I would have to be paid in advance for the out-of-pocket costs of the search. I use a Washington firm and, in view of his age, although I didn't mention that, I didn't want to be stuck for the cost of the search."

"He paid you right away?" Warren asked.

"He took a wad of ten-dollar bills out of his pocket and counted them twice. He must have saved for a year."

"Did he always pay you in cash?"

"For out-of-pocket expenses, yes. I ordered two more searches at his insistence, one about six months ago and the other about two months ago."

"All negative?"

"There was absolutely no prior art. Kassel had definitely hit on a new principle and devised a practical embodiment of it."

"Kassel was not an engineer, was he?" Warren asked.

"He was a high-school graduate and had been a machinist for fifty years. Many inventions are made, even today, by people with no technical background at all, even less than Kassel."

"You said a new principle was involved, Mr. Slowicki."

"In loudspeakers, yes; not a new scientific law. In fact, anyone who knew the most elementary electricity and magnetism, high-school physics, could have invented this speaker. No new technology was involved, just a new way of putting known technology together. You could have done it, if you had the inventive flash of insight."

Warren returned to his original line of questioning. "Did you ever wonder how he got the money for the patent application? Did he pay your fee in cash, too?"

"Many old people have a source of income off the books, especially people with a good trade. But I realized that he was probably using all he had earned and saved, so, out of pity, I agreed that my fee would be paid just prior to filing. He did pay the costs of the patent drafting, copying, typing, mailing, and so forth."

"Were you the one who sent him to Hamilcar?"

"I knew of Hamilcar, of course, but I had never done business with them. I always advise my attic inventors to find a licensee as soon as possible and conclude a deal with him. Normally, I would help the inventor to find someone to license, show him how to use *Thomas' Register* and similar sources, but Kassel was such a suspicious type that I didn't want him to think I was pushing any particular manufacturer. I told him to work from the Yellow Pages. He seems to have made a proper choice."

"Is it customary for you to represent the inventor in licensing negotiations?"

"Sometimes. I try not to, especially now, and there are some good local attorneys I recommend who are experienced in this kind of work. But Kassel's nature was such, he had grown to trust me a little, that I felt it would be better to represent him myself. Besides, in the past couple of months, I got the impression he was running out of money and would not have enough to pay a retainer to a new attorney."

"How did Kassel come to you?" Warren asked. "I checked the phone book and all you have is a listing. You don't advertise, do you?"

"As I said, I'm trying to retire. Kassel worked for a firm, Nassau Model Fabricators, that was one of the companies I recommended to inventors who could afford to have a model made. It's very useful, very important, to make a model. There are several reasons. First and foremost, a patent is issued to whoever does the first reduction to practice. There are only two ways to do this: One is to file an application for patent, and two is to make a working model. Second, when you make the model, it may not work the way you thought, or you may discover an improvement, or a necessary modification that you want to incorporate in the application. And third, it's a lot better, when you want to license or sell an invention, to show a working model than a drawing."

"Did you know Kassel when you worked with Nassau Model?"

"No. I never visited Nassau Model, but that's how he knew of me and why he chose me, he said. They did beautiful work, and I'm sure Kassel was one of the reasons for this."

"I'd like to talk to Nassau Model Fabricators. What's the name and phone number of the owner?"

"They went out of business two years ago, when Sam Moscow died."

"Did Kassel make the model of his new speaker?" Warren asked.

"I'm sure he did, but as I said, we spoke very little. I can't imagine him letting anyone else do it. After all, he used to be in the model business. I can't even imagine him letting anyone see the sketches. It took fifteen minutes for me to persuade him that for me to file a patent for him I'd have to know how the invention worked."

"Did you hear the speaker?"

"I never even saw it. He told me he had the model in his shopping bag, and gave me some Polaroid photos of it as proof that the model existed, both in its enclosure and with the guts exposed, but that's all."

"Was there any difference between the drawings and the photos?"

"Nothing significant. You must understand the psychology of an attic inventor. He dreams about his invention, sometimes for years, to the point where every screw is real. He changes it and improves it over the years until, when it comes to me, it is absolutely perfect."

"But sometimes it isn't perfect, is it?"

"Many times. Often it doesn't work, can't work, violates a basic law of physics. And even more often, it's been patented already or is unpatentable. Most often, it has so little economic value you try to discourage the inventor. You never can. But also sometimes, it's a basic invention, one that founds an industry. Like xerography, instant photography, solid-state devices. You never know what walks through a patent attorney's door. I love this business. It's full of surprises."

"And you feel this speaker will really revolutionize the hi-fi industry?"

"I've never heard it, but from the interest expressed by Hamilcar, it must sound very good. The principle is certainly ingenious and simple. So with the caveats I expressed before, I think it *will* revolutionize the industry. Kassel's name will go down in history."

"Why didn't Kassel allow us to examine the speaker?" Warren asked.

"I really tried to explain it to him, showed him standard confidential disclosure agreements. Nothing worked. He was adamant. He would not, under any conditions, allow anyone to see the inside of the speaker until the patent application had been filed. Not even the sketches."

"Because he had once been cheated, you said. Did he ever tell you the details of that incident?"

"Barely mentioned it. I told you, we exchanged very few words."

Warren seemed to be finished, so I got down to business. "When are you filing, Lou?"

"In two days we should be ready, three at the most. It depends on how many mistakes I find in the proofreading and the checking."

"Lou, there's no delicate way to put this, and please don't read any pressure into this. In two or three days we'll all be allowed to take the speaker apart and see the patent application. As of right now we are practically your clients. Can you let me see the application?"

Slowicki looked embarrassed. "I'm sorry, Mr. Baer, I can't, according to the agreements that were signed. Please understand my position and be patient another few days."

I understood, shook hands, and left. Warren sat at the wheel of the car for a moment, then said, "Let's go talk to Thanatopoulos again. Maybe he can give us another lead to the other guy Kassel worked for."

"How will that help?"

"I don't know. It may be useless or he might be the key to the puzzle. I just want to have all the information possible before I really begin thinking about the problem."

"Up to now you haven't been thinking?"

"Not comprehensively, just in parts. What else have I got to do today?"

"You were supposed to check to see if there were any other entrances to the anechoic chamber."

"Okay, I'll do that right after we track down Kassel's other employer. I'll dump you off at the office first."

"Never. I'll go with you." There was no way I was going to let Warren go anywhere alone, much less into the Hamilcar plant where the murderer was waiting. Not after my good buddy, Sergeant Palmieri, had set Warren up as the decoy goat.

XX

Democritos Thanatopoulos was even less happy to see us than the last time. "What the hell you want now, huh?" he asked. "I told you before, I got nobody working off the books. You want to check, come any night, even Sunday."

I knew for sure that for the next month or two there'd be no more night work, but after he felt the heat had died down, he'd be doing it again. His business was too obviously marginal to take a cut in income. When it came down to it, with the choice of his family not eating or his breaking the law, I knew what choice I would make.

"We're not interested in your operation, Mr. Thanatopoulos," Warren said. "We only want information about Walter Kassel."

"He never did no work here. Prove he did."

"I don't have to prove anything," Warren said. "I'm not accusing you of anything. But you knew him, you called him."

"We used to play dominoes at night. Prove we didn't."

"I don't care what you did. What I want to know is who else he worked for. Do you know?"

"Why you want to say 'who else'? You trying to say he worked here off the books?"

Warren tried the same technique that had worked before. "All right. If a man his age, a machinist, wanted to

123

pick up a few bucks off the books, at night, who in Nassau County could he have worked for?"

Thanatopoulos gave a short bark of a laugh. "You got the Yellow Pages? Pick a company. You think there's a million good machinists around? Old-fashioned machinists who know one end of a micrometer from the other? Hah!"

"But you don't know who?"

"I never know if he *ever* work for anybody. All we talk is dominoes. He was on Social Security, so how could he work? You work on Social Security, they take away half the money."

"How did you meet Kassel that you became so friendly with him? To play dominoes with at night, I mean."

"We used to work in the same company, Nassau Model. When the boss dies, I start my own business, Kassel retire. We play dominoes lunchtime. I always win."

"Do you still see some of the other employees of Nassau Model?"

He grew stiff again. "Only to play dominoes with. You can check. Nobody tell you different."

I figured it was time for me to step in. Not to knock Warren, but there are certain things they don't teach in college. "Demo," I said, smiling in a certain way that the right type of businessman would understand, "just in case you know some of the other old guys who used to play dominoes at night, just in case one of them knows who Kassel worked for when he wasn't playing dominoes here, I'd like to know. Got it?"

He looked me straight in the eye. "It could take a lot of time, I'm pretty busy. And I don't know if I remember. I got to think a lot. Maybe make a lot of phone calls."

I looked straight back at him. "I understand it might take a lot of time, so if you should phone me the name and address, that's all I want, a name and an address, I don't even want to know who remembered what, I would really appreciate it. Very much."

"How much?"

"One bill to the guy who remembers, five bills to the guy who phones me."

"Cash?"

"I said bills, not checks."

"Not on the phone. In person, so we could shake hands."

"Okay. In person."

"If nobody knows? There's still expenses."

"Don't I look over twenty-one, Demo?" His face fell. "Okay, here's twenty, for expenses, win, lose or draw. And the five and one is on top of that. But that's it. Any jacking up and there'll be real trouble. Here's my card. It only works for the next two days, though. After that, don't bother calling me."

My language he understood. I could see Warren didn't like it, but what the hell. Compared to the construction business, this was peanuts. Someday I'd tell him the story of Alexander and the Gordian knot. One of my favorites. We left.

Suddenly Warren spoke up. "Why didn't you offer him more money?"

"That was just the right amount for him," I said. "More would have made him suspicious, made the deal look dangerous."

"But five hundred dollars? It's not a really big incentive."

"For you, no; for him, yes. And it was six hundred. You think he was going to give any to the guy who told him where Kassel worked? And you're looking at it wrong. Six hundred in cash is twelve hundred taxable; the net profit on a twelve-thousand-dollar order for Thanatopoulos. All for making a few phone calls, without investment or risk. Believe me, when he finds the factory, he'll call me first thing. There aren't many places in Nassau County where Kassel could have worked nights, off the books, which are on a bus line from the Mineola terminal, and Thanatopoulos knows them all."

We drove to the Hamilcar plant to check the number of

holes in the concrete box. There was still no one following us, keeping an eye on Warren. Either I didn't read Palmieri right, or he didn't give a damn for Warren. Or, and I didn't really believe this, he got a sudden attack of morals and wasn't going to use Warren as a staked-out goat for his tiger trap. Nah, not possible. You don't get to be a sergeant, not even in a nice place like Nassau County, by being soft.

XXI

Warren went over every square foot of the exterior of the anechoic chamber. It really was completely separated from the rest of the structure, the way Fred Gorman had said, with enough clearance at the floor of the second level so you could look down and see that there was no opening within the depth of the floor system. The only part we couldn't get to was the top of the concrete box, which was about twenty feet up from the upper floor, just below the bottom of the exposed steel bar joists supporting the roof.

Tony Russo was walking past, so I grabbed him. "Do you have any ladders," I asked, "or extension ladders, long enough to get me to the top there?"

"No," he answered. "What do you want to go up there for?"

"To see if there are any openings a murderer could use."

"You still on that? Forget it, Ed. That's solid reinforced concrete, over a foot thick. I saw it poured."

"I have to see for myself, Tony. How about hooking together a couple of those ladders you have in the warehouse area?"

"No good. They're made for hanging, not bending. But—" he thought for a moment—"if you really want to get up there, I can do it for you. I'll send up two of the ladders, make that three, and a couple of my warehouse men."

127

"Not Cuccio, I hope."

He smiled. "Would I do that to you, Ed? After you were going to arrange it so I got killed? Okay, okay, a couple of good men. But you got to supervise them, I'm too busy to screw around with your games."

"What do I do?"

"Have them wire together two ladders, side by side, so you'll have enough width to be stable; one is too narrow by itself. Then lean the pair against the side of the chamber. You and one of my guys hold the ladders steady. Make sure the flat ends are against the concrete, not the hooks. The other of my guys climbs up. Hand him the third ladder, hooks up. He reaches up with it, it's light, and hooks it to the bottom chord of one of the steel bar joists, so it hangs down. Climb that, and you're on top of the chamber. Be careful, don't swing the ladder too much when you climb it. I'll send up a hundred-foot extension with a strong light, too."

"Will it hold my weight?" I asked. "Warren isn't used to high places."

"Are you kidding? In tension, it should hold a ton, easy. When you're finished, tell my guys to put everything back where it came from and go back to what they were doing."

Warren objected, but I went up anyway. Heights never bothered me, and I'm used to ladders. I didn't want Warren to freeze hanging on a ladder, twenty feet in the air. I've seen it happen before, and it's very hard to get the guy down. And he's changed by the experience. Badly.

It cost me a suit, but I found there was only solid concrete up there. And lots of dust and dirt and odds and ends left over from construction. Sloppy building. When I was a general contractor, I always turned over a building spotless. A matter of pride, which they don't seem to have too much of these days. Not that I would, but I bet if I went back in business, I'd wipe out half the contractors on the Island in two years.

Warren had been doing some thinking while I was crawling around on top of the anechoic chamber. He wouldn't tell me what it was about; he wanted to talk to Carter Hamilton again.

Carter was annoyed to see us, but I insisted. We went into his office and shut the door. Warren's approach was mild and friendly. "When you first started Hamilcar, where did you work, Mr. Hamilton?"

"In the garage of my house."

"Was your first design the one you eventually manufactured as the HHF-1?"

"Of course not. The basic concept worked, but a production model is the result of a great many revisions and compromises."

"How long did it take you to make your first rough model?"

"Including the false starts, about three months."

"You did all of this yourself?"

"Completely. It was rather crude. I had to use existing drivers and commercial crossovers, but I could tell I had a good speaker. I bought a signal generator and a sound level meter, and the test results agreed with my ears."

"That's when you decided to form Hamilcar Hi-Fi?"

"Yes. I brought in Fred, who had roomed with me in school, and John, who was working for a kit company. I met him at an Audio Society meeting and liked him. Fred brought in George, from Harvard Business, and John brought in Russo. We looked around and stole Rollie from a retail chain. We each put in what we had, mostly my money, and you know the rest."

"Did Borovic and Russo help you design the production model?"

"Yes," Carter said flatly. "I couldn't have done it without them. My basic concept was sound, but at that time I didn't have the faintest idea of what went into a production model."

"Have you done any design since?"

"That's John's job. I have enough to do administering the company and setting policy."

"He really messed up the HHF-2, didn't he?"

"He's not alone. We all agreed we wanted a cheap model with a rock-and-roll sound. Don't forget, he also designed the HHF-1A, a real improvement."

"You manufacture your own drivers and crossovers now. Did you do it then?"

"No. That is, we were able to use an existing tweeter and midrange off the shelf, but there was no woofer that met our requirements."

"Couldn't you get one made by a driver manufacturer?"

"Sure, but for any of them to design and produce a woofer exactly to our specs, and who knew how long we would be in business, they wanted a lot of money in advance. Almost all the capital we had left."

"So you designed and built your own woofer?"

"I did the basic design, John perfected it, and Tony made it economical. It's what made us. Anyone can turn out a pretty good tweeter cheap, and even a fairly good midrange. And if you want to spend the time and money, you can make a very good crossover, practically right out of the handbook. But a woofer in an acoustic suspension speaker, that's hard."

"Did you make it yourself then?"

"The first models? How could we? We went to a good machine shop."

"Do you remember the name?"

"That was ten years ago. More. Nassau Tool and Die, something like that."

"Nassau Model Fabricators?"

Carter smiled in recognition. "That's it. Sam Moscow. Charged heavy, but did a good job. One of the few shops on the Island that worked in any material: ferrous, nonferrous, wood, plastic, anything."

"Did you ever visit his shop?"

"We all did, at one time or another. That is, Russo, Borovic, and I did, regularly, the others, once or twice. There were always decisions to be made."

Without changing his quiet tone, Warren said, "Was that when you first met Walter Kassel?"

Carter looked stunned for a moment, then he recovered. "That's it. I knew when I first saw him that I had seen him before, but I couldn't remember where. It was ten years ago. He had gotten very thin, since."

"Had you ever spoken to him at Nassau Model?"

"No, he was just a machinist. Sam was the mechanical wizard."

"He said nothing to you when he came here?"

"Maybe he didn't remember. He was pretty old."

"Do you think that's why he came to Hamilcar first?"

"It's very likely. We had a good relationship with Sam Moscow. We paid our bills on time and didn't give him impossible deadlines."

"Russo and Borovic didn't recognize him either?"

"Evidently not, otherwise they would have said something. We never addressed him by name in the old days; he was just one of the machinists that worked on our woofer. I probably wouldn't recognize any of Moscow's other men either, if I met one on the street, unless you told me where he worked then."

"You didn't quarrel with Kassel when he was at Nassau Model, did you? Criticize his work?"

"I told you, I never spoke to him. And the work was very good. Sam was an old-timer, a perfectionist."

"Did you ever use them again?"

"After we built the factory we didn't have to. We had our own shop and it was quicker and cheaper to use our own men."

"You now make all your drivers?"

"Even the tweeters. It costs a few cents more to make them than to buy them, but our quality control is tops. We've built up a good reputation and we mean to keep it."

"Would you please call Russo and Borovic on the intercom to come here?" Warren asked. "I want to ask them about Nassau Model."

Borovic arrived first, Russo a couple of minutes later. Carter started to speak, but Warren stopped him. "Did you know," he asked the two bluntly, "that Walter Kassel worked on the first model of the HHF-1 when he was with Nassau Model?" They both looked dumb for a moment, then Borovic spoke. "Sure. I knew he looked familiar. That's from where."

"He's the guy who worked on the shaping of the pole pieces," Russo said. "I remember. But he changed. How did you know?" he asked Warren.

"Checked around," Warren said calmly, looking pleased. "Did any of the others ever see him there? Why don't you check, Mr. Hamilton?"

Hamilton got on the intercom and turned it up so we all could hear. In turn, Rollie said, "Sure I went there. To ask when it would be ready. But I only spoke to Moscow." George said, "I had to spot-check the labor and material costs, and I saw all of them." Fred said, "I went a few times. It's my job to know everything that goes on. But I didn't speak to the machinists." None of them remembered seeing Kassel.

The three executives in the office reminisced for a few minutes, reliving those first exciting, frightening days. Then Carter turned to Warren. A good sign, that he should recognize that Warren was leading the investigation. "This is very interesting, Warren," Carter said, "but how does it help? That we had a slight relationship with Kassel in the old days is clear, and it may be more than coincidental. I'm sure, now, that's why he approached us, which is all to the good. But I can't believe this sheds any light on his death. We hardly knew him ten years ago, and certainly had no hard feelings toward him then, or any kind of feelings, for that matter. Whatever his reason for being killed, I'm sure it doesn't relate to that past."

"You're probably right, Mr. Hamilton," Warren said, "but it's an added bit of information. You never know how it may fit in. I'm going to give it to Sergeant Palmieri. Maybe he can figure out a connection."

"Speaking of Palmieri," Hamilton said to me, "did you tell him to let us into the chamber?"

"He said he'd probably unseal it in a few more days," I evaded. I was relieved. Evidently Palmieri decided not to use Warren as a decoy. So far.

Carter looked at Russo. "Do you realize what this means, Tony?"

Tony looked as though he was swallowing a big lump. "Sure. I got to kill myself, make up two additional days. All right, I'll do it. But I don't want to hear any bullshit from George about the overtime." He turned on me. "And from you, Ed, I don't want to hear any questions about my unaudited expenses, you know what I mean? Because I'll be taking care of my shop stewards and the business agent and pushing quotas up and passing on bonuses to the good producers off the books. Is that clear?" He looked as though he was ready to take us all on. He stalked out of the room, but at the door stopped and said, quietly, "And once, just one lousy time, I want to hea· somebody say, 'Good job, Tony,' instead of all the bitching I get from all sides all the time. I don't work just for the money, you know." He slammed the door.

Warren and I left; no point hanging around. We went home and Warren called Palmieri about the Nassau Model connection he had found. Palmieri had nothing to report.

I didn't know what else I could do, so I told Warren I was going to lie down, take a nap before supper, let my subconscious work on solving the problem of how to murder Kassel in the dead room.

Warren fooled me. I thought he was going to work on his book, which he hadn't touched in three days. He told me that was at a dead end on the means of killing, so he was going to analyze motives.

That gave me an idea, so I called Iris Guralnik at home from my bedroom. She couldn't cancel any more patients, clients, this week, but she could meet me at the same Howard Johnson's at nine-fifteen this evening. I wouldn't tell her what it was for; it would do her good to wonder.

I couldn't believe it, but I was looking forward to talking to her.

XXII

"How do you explain going out at night to your husband?" I asked, after the waitress brought the coffee and Danish.

"I don't," Iris said complacently, taking a big bite. "Let him sweat. Makes him more appreciative."

"Until you wake up one day with your throat cut?"

"Nah, not Marvin. He knows I'm a good girl."

"Isn't he dying of curiosity?"

"Sure. But if I tell him what I'm doing, he'll mess things up. Not that he doesn't like Warren, but he thinks Lee is too good for anyone less than the Dictator of the Universe. Typical father syndrome, with a beautiful daughter."

"And you?" I asked. "You think she isn't worth an emperor? Or at least a billionaire?"

"What I want is for her to have happiness, not money."

"Money buys health, love, and happiness, Iris. Or at least takes away the money worries so you can concentrate on what is important."

"How many rich people do you know, Ed, who are happy? Or who don't worry about money? What would make Lee happy is lots of kids and a loving husband. Warren. So is that what you want to report on?"

"To begin with. He's really taken over the investigation. I did what you said and it worked. Also, he's not so fresh anymore."

"Stick with me, kid," she said with a shyster-agent leer, "and you'll be wearing zircons. You're getting free what people pay me good money for."

"As a potential in-law, Iris, you have to give me a discount."

"*When* we're in-laws, you get ten percent off."

"Twenty. Retroactive. Now let me tell you something you'll really love." I told her in great detail, blow by blow, how Warren had handled the Cuccio problem. She really enjoyed the story. "See," she said, "I told you if you let him have his head, he'd show what he could do. What else happened in the last couple of days?"

I filled her in on everything, especially how Warren had tracked down the connection from ten years ago between Hamilcar and Kassel. "I don't think it has any bearing on the case," I told her, "but you never know."

"The important thing is," she said, "that he accomplished something no one else had thought of, not even the police. He's at the stage where he needs a few more wins, Ed, so he can become independent of you."

"I'm willing, Iris, but how? That's the problem. We've divided up the work. I'm trying to figure out how the murder was committed, he's trying to figure out why."

"Have you come up with anything, Ed?"

"Zilch. I'm ready to go down to the morgue to see if Kassel's really there. As far as I can tell, there was no way to kill him in the dead room."

"What about motive? Did any of them have a strong reason to kill Kassel?"

"Are you kidding? They all hated him. A couple of them even had two motives."

"Who?"

"Carter, for one. And Gorman. George Sambur. Russo. And Borovic. And Rollie Franklin. Hell, they all had two motives. That I know of. The trouble is, I don't know if any of them had enough incentive to commit murder."

"Did Warren mention any ideas he had?"

"If he had even an approach, the slightest, he would have tried it out on me, gotten my reaction."

"So that's what I'm here for?" she said shrewdly.

"At least to figure out a place to start. Motives are your business, Iris."

"I don't work miracles, Ed," she warned. "But what the hell, let's give it a try. With the understanding that, if we come up with anything good, you put the idea in Warren's head very discreetly, so it seems to be his own."

"I can be subtle if I have to; you know me, Iris."

"Damn right, Ed, that's why I said it. Okay, tell me what you think about each of the suspects. And for God's sake, don't try to be objective. Give me your feelings, an honest reaction, and I'll weigh it with what I know about your character."

I wasn't sure how to take that, but I started anyway. "Carter Hamilton. Although his father wasn't as rich as Carter thought, he acted like a rich man's son trying to be a hippie. He's in his mid-thirties, but still has long hair and a beard. Wears overalls and sneakers. Good administrator and a good technical mind. Potentially a good business-man and probably will be a very effective president, now that he's been so close to losing it all. A little childish, sometimes, but doesn't let it interfere with his business decisions. Unmarried, but living with a nice girl. He's sort of puritanical in his private life; no smoking, no drinking; Granola type."

"What's he like physically?"

"Slim. Seems to be healthy. I get the impression he hikes a lot and grows his own organic vegetables."

"You don't like him, do you, Ed?"

"Not particularly. He seems to still live in what I call The Phony Generation, the one where kids who didn't have the faintest idea of what it was like, took on the outward characteristics of poor Southern black sharecrop-

pers. Their intentions might have been good, but what
they missed completely was that they had a choice: They
could always wire home for money, the real black kids
couldn't. It makes all the difference in the world. It's between playing at and for real."

"Why would Carter Hamilton want to kill Kassel?"

"Lots of reasons. He makes more money, for one. Not
much, because I'm fixing it so Kassel's money goes to his
heirs, if any, but Carter once thought that he could get it
all for the company. Then, he wants to get credit for the
Kassel design. The way other people see Carter seems to
be very important to him. Warren thinks Carter's trying to
prove to his father, his dead father, that he's a success."

"It's a pity he couldn't do it while his father was alive,
isn't it?"

"Don't rub it in, Iris. I understood that the minute Warren mentioned it."

"So what did you do about it?"

"I couldn't do anything right at that moment; it would
have looked phony. But at the proper time . . ."

"Make sure it's soon, Ed. Very soon."

"I know. But I can't just manufacture a situation."

"It doesn't need a situation; you could just say the magic
words anytime. But you wouldn't be Ed Baer if you could
just say, 'I love you,' at will."

"If you could just say that, like you say 'Hello,' it
wouldn't mean anything."

"Well, maybe, for some people . . . Ah, what the hell,
no sense in belaboring the point. When you're ready, you'll
say it. Meanwhile, let's get back to Carter Hamilton.
Would it be a disaster for him if Hamilcar Hi-Fi failed?"

"Absolutely. It's not just the money, although I think
Carter would find it very hard to work for someone else.
He might enjoy going up to Vermont and working a small
farm, for a while at least, but it would be the loss of the
company that would kill him. It was the first thing he

accomplished by himself. Even with his father's money, it was quite a trick to start a company at twenty-five and succeed. He's very proud of that, and he has a right to be. Also, his first speaker, inventing it, and getting it accepted—I know he's proud of that."

"Would Kassel's death hurt the company?"

"On balance, I'd say yes. It's true the old man was a pain to work with, and very slow, but it was his baby. When it came time to make the modifications in the production model, he'd be worth ten times his fee. Also, he was an expert machinist. He might be able to advise Russo on production techniques."

"Other than the Nassau Model connection, do you know of any contact between Hamilton and Kassel?"

"No, and I was watching. I think Carter was genuinely surprised when I reminded him of it."

Iris studied me for a minute. "Carter Hamilton is your choice for the killer, isn't he?" I nodded, surprised. "Why?" she asked.

I had to think about this. "Prejudice," I admitted. "That's all I can come up with. A rich man's son. What I had to kill myself for, deprive my family, was handed to him on a silver platter."

"Warren's a rich man's son," she pointed out.

"Warren's nice. He worked every summer as a laborer."

"I'll bet Carter's father thought he was nice, too."

"What can I say, Iris? You asked how I felt."

"And I found out. Who's the next suspect?"

"Fred Gorman, the executive V.P. Tall, slim, blond, handsome. Very smart, very efficient. Wears a full business uniform all the time. He has to be burning that, although they started as roommates in college, Carter is now president and Fred is not. Fred has a lot less technical expertise than Hamilton, but he could step into Carter's shoes in one minute."

"So what's his motive?"

"If Carter hangs for murder, Gorman would be the logical new president. It wouldn't give him any more stock, but it would bring a sizable increase in salary and the title. This, at his age, could open some really big jobs in some big companies five years down the line."

"But only if Carter leaves."

"Right. If some evidence suddenly turned up implicating Carter in the killing, I'd check out Gorman very carefully. The trouble is, there's no evidence against anybody."

"Do you like Gorman, Ed?"

"Not really. He's a little too smooth; makes me feel as though he's weighing what he says before he says it. But I don't dislike him and he'd make a terrific president."

"Could he have killed Kassel?"

"Easily, if he had anything to gain. He's by far the smartest of the lot, sharper even than Sambur, the controller. But what's his motive? If he wanted to sabotage Carter, there are a hundred easier ways to do it, ways that would be less harmful to the company than killing Kassel, ways much less dangerous to Gorman himself. And to tell you the truth, I haven't seen the slightest sign of Gorman's undercutting Hamilton. Everything he does seems to be for the good of the company."

"Could killing Kassel be for the good of the company?"

"I don't see how. Do you?"

"I don't know enough to say. Actually, I don't know anything. All I'm doing with you is what I do with my clients, getting you to tell yourself, out loud, what you already know. Would you believe that most people *know* what's troubling them? And that it takes a lot of skill and talent to get them to see it?"

"Are you telling me, Iris, that I know who the killer is and how he did it?"

"Probably. You just don't know you know. Keep talking. Tell me about the controller."

"George Sambur? Pudgy with a will of iron. If he's right, you can't move him. He's had run-ins with every executive in the place, and he always wins. Does numbers in his head faster than a computer. The only way to handle him is to tell him, firmly, what the policy is. He'll implement it like a robot. No heart, no compassion, no human emotions. Except maybe eating."

"You don't like him?"

"What's to like? I'll bet when he goes home, he plays games against himself on a computer all night long."

"So why keep him?"

"He's the best. You want to know which retail outlet is going to sell how many HHF-1As next Washington's Birthday sale, he'll give you the answer in seconds. Russo spends one dollar over projection, he gets a memo from George. Franklin pays fifteen cents more for a bottle of Scotch in the hospitality suite at a show, Sambur sends him a list of cut-rate liquor stores in that city."

"I take it he's not well loved in the company."

"Respected. That's as far as I go. And he does make the finances work. He doesn't object to spending a buck to make two, like so many controllers do. He's just waiting at the door when you bring it back to make sure it isn't $1.99."

"Would he kill Kassel?"

"If George found his mother had cost the company seven cents over budget, he'd wire her to a computer."

"Did Kassel do anything wrong financially?"

"Not as far as we know, although he may have been stalling to keep getting fees. The speaker sounds great, they say, the tests are better than expected, and the patent lawyer says the application looks very sound. All Kassel has seen from us is four hundred a week, as contracted. And he's been working every day for it, full days. Meticulously."

"The wasted time and money doesn't seem like much of a motive. And the delay in completing the tests affected all the executives, not just Sambur."

"Sambur has one motive the others don't. Kassel was

blackmailing Georgie boy. He threatened Sambur to take an extra month for the testing if George opened his mouth about the test delays."

"Do you see that as a real threat to Sambur? Something to kill Kassel over?"

"Not really, Iris, although Sambur might have thought so. All George had to do was keep his mouth shut for a few more days. Kassel was on his last test, there was no way he could delay completion for another month."

"Kassel could have delayed the filing of the patent application, couldn't he? By not signing the papers?"

"Maybe he could, but it would have been a breach of the contract. I don't think Slowicki would have let him get away with it."

"So tell me about one of the others."

"Rollie Franklin, sales manager. Nervous, fat, high-energy, always on, a worrier. Definite type A personality. Would parade naked down Northern Boulevard if it would increase sales one percent. Always trying to beat last week, last month, last year, you name it."

"Would he kill?"

"Only for something important. Like if the retailer put the Hamilcar display in second position."

"What motive would he have to kill Kassel?"

"If he thought it would mean making the Winter Consumer Electronics Show on time, he'd kill everybody in the place. And be sure he was doing the right thing."

"Unstable?"

"Completely. But that's normal for a man his age about to go on the breadline; he's just turned forty."

"Change of life?"

"Rollie goes through a change of life twice a day."

"Talk seriously, Ed. Could Rollie Franklin have killed Kassel?"

"I am talking seriously, Iris. Of all the executives, Rollie would need the least reason, from an outsider's point of view, to kill Kassel."

"You said they all had two motives. What's Rollie's?"

I told her all about Rollie's mother. "Rollie sounds like a very disturbed man," she said. "Wouldn't you put him at the head of the list?"

"He could also be a good Jewish son, Iris. Giving up your life for someone you love is not necessarily a sickness. The way Rollie responded when I said Kassel was killing his mother, I would have said the same thing myself if I was in that position."

"Are you sure an executive did it?" she asked.

"Has to be. I'm betting my business and Warren's future on it, that's how sure I am."

"Do you really want to find the killer, Ed?"

That really stopped me. Iris was even shrewder than I had given her credit for before, and that was plenty. I had to say it. "Yes and no. No, because it has to hurt the company. Yes, because it's the right thing to do. But I'm committed, Iris, I really am."

"I still think you're ambivalent, but let's keep talking. Who's next?"

"John Borovic, chief engineer. Big, looks like a truck driver, sort of square. The kind who, in my day, if you asked him two times two, would whip out the slide rule and come up with 3.99 plus or minus .01. Jealous of Kassel, I can smell it. Did a good job on the HHF-1, a lousy job on the HHF-2, although maybe that wasn't all his fault, and then improved the HHF-1 to the 1A, a damn good job. I think he's torn between wanting the new speaker to succeed, so he can make money, and having it self-destruct, so he can go back to being one of the famous designers again. But as I read him, when we open the box, he'll work out a dozen ways to improve it that no one else in the industry could do, and he'll work night and day to bring it in on time."

"He hated Kassel?"

"Naturally. I'm a half-assed engineer myself, and I'm dying of curiosity to know what's inside, what the new principle is. Imagine how John feels. He'd probably give a year off his life to be working on the new speaker now."

"Would he kill Kassel to see the new speaker a day earlier?"

"Sure. With his bare hands. But not in the anechoic chamber where the police would keep him from the speaker for a couple of days, at least. If Kassel had lived, the probability is that the last tests would have been finished three days ago and we'd be filed by now. As it is, we can't see the inside of the speaker or the patent application for two or three more days. Right now is not the time to tease or annoy the animals. Can you imagine what it must feel like to John to have a mechanic come up with the speaker of the century?"

"Do you think John did it?"

"If Kassel was mugged in Mineola on the way home, and the speaker was missing, I'd go right to John's office. He'd be there, taking the bloodstained speaker apart, begging me not to tell the police until he was finished redesigning it. But in the anechoic chamber? Never."

"Jealousy and pride can be very strong motives, Ed. Don't discount them."

"I'm not counting John out yet, Iris. But how would killing Kassel gain Borovic respect as a designer?"

"I don't know. I'm just trying to stimulate you. What about the production manager?"

"Tony Russo. Short, dark, excitable. He'll get a heart attack before he's fifty, if his ulcer doesn't perforate first. Probably threatened to kill Carter more often than he threatened Kassel. Overworked, overharassed, and a real pro. I could see him tearing out Kassel's throat with his teeth in front of everybody, sure, but sneaking into the chamber? That doesn't seem to be his style."

"In a fit of anger?"

"Anybody could kill anybody in a fit of anger, Iris, you and me included. But this killing was planned. I just don't see Tony as a cold-blooded killer."

"He's capable of planning it, isn't he?"

"Tony? Oh, sure. He'd be the best at that, a real improvisor, a quick thinker, practical. He figured out in one minute how to get me to the top of the chamber. If anyone could plot the perfect crime, he could."

"You told me before that Russo said he was going to kill Kassel before Kassel killed him."

"Kassel wasn't trying to kill Russo; *Russo* is trying to kill Russo; his temper, I mean."

"So you don't think Russo did it?"

"I'm not ruling out any of them, Iris, but you asked for my personal feelings."

"Could that be because Tony Russo is so much like you?"

"Like me? That's crazy. When did you ever see me lose my cool?"

"Every time we play golf. Once you did it four times in one round. It could kill you, Ed. Think about it."

"You want me to go to a shrink? Is that what you're saying?"

"If that's the only way, yes. But I think you can handle it yourself, now that you know. You decide."

"Why are you so concerned about me, Iris? Half the time we're talking, I get the feeling you're not listening to what I say, you're watching how I say it."

"You're partly right, Ed; I'm doing both. And I'll tell you something else I don't want talked around. Marvin is a dentist, a plain dentist. Not a periodontist, not an orthodontist, not a specialist of any kind. He makes money only when his hands are in somebody's mouth. There are only so many hours in a day before the back gives out. Other than the Keogh plan and a small checking account, every penny we have is invested in Nassau Venture Capital. So stay healthy, Ed. We need you."

"That's stupid, Iris. You should diversify. Is that why Marvin is so worried all the time, asking too many questions about the business?"

"That's why, Ed. And we don't want to diversify. We think you're the best. Just stay alive and see your grandchildren grow up. All six, all blonds."

"You're telling me Lee doesn't bring Warren a big dowry?"

"Not a cent. Let the young couple have the fun of building together."

"I hate to disillusion you, Iris, but on his twenty-fifth birthday, I'm executor, he gets half of NVC. Thelma left it all to him. We agreed."

"You mean he'll be rich? Can't you delay it some way?"

"No way, Iris. But he's a good boy; it won't hurt him."

"You may be right, but it's bad to have too much money too soon."

"You want me to start pushing Judy Fein again?"

"Don't make jokes, Ed, I'm serious. Which reminds me, you and Warren are invited for supper a week from Sunday. Cocktails and snacks at six, dinner at eight. Lee will be back from school and she'll cook it all. It'll open your eyes."

"I'd love to come, but I don't have . . . I'll have to come alone, if it doesn't spoil your arrangements for dinner. It's only six months, Iris; I'm not ready yet."

"I know you're not, and if I leave you alone, you never will be. So *I'll* tell *you* when you're ready and, if you learn to control yourself, I'll even tell you *who*."

"Already you're running my life, Iris, and we're not even related yet?"

"Thelma did it, and you loved it. And, whether you know it or not, you need it. Here's what to do for next Sunday. You'll pick up Dottie Lesser at her house at five-forty-five. Sport clothes, nothing formal. Warren will drive his own car so he and Lee can take off after dinner and be by themselves."

"Dottie Lesser? Barry died only four months ago. Does she really want to go out on a date?"

"She has to. It's important. Don't worry, it's all arranged."

"But I don't— Since I got married, I didn't fool around, Iris. Not even once. I wouldn't know what to do."

"Act natural. Tell her how nice she looks. Be attentive, but not too obvious. And talk to her. About anything that interests you."

"What about taking her home, Iris? I don't want to start something, or lead her on or anything."

"Neither does she, really. See her to the door, tell her you had a great time with her, that you hope to see her again sometime, kiss her goodnight lightly, and go. Don't go in with her, even if she invites you. Make an excuse. Unless you really want to and she really wants to, that is. But you won't. She's not the one for you or you for her."

"Then why?"

"Practice, practice, practice, Ed. And Dottie needs a lift."

"All right, I'll do it, and I'll enjoy it, too. Dottie is a nice woman. But what about Warren? If this case isn't settled by then, he may be . . . he may lose confidence in himself again."

"So settle it. Solve the murder."

"Just like that? That's funny, Iris, very funny. You didn't tell me a damn thing. I wanted you to analyze the motives for me."

"I did what I had to do: I asked the right questions. You put everything together neatly. Now all you have to do is think. So go home and think. Don't forget to tell Warren to keep next Sunday open."

All I had to do was think? If this is what a shrink does,

who needs it? In the days of the rubber hose, we didn't have such problems. This is progress?

Well, I'd talk it over with Warren tomorrow morning. Maybe his way of analysis was better. If he could write a book on how we know what we know, it should be easy for him to figure out who done it.

XXIII

Although it was late, Warren was still up. Not working on his book, just staring at the wall.

"Can't sleep?" I asked.

"If someone is murdered," he said slowly, "there has to be a reason."

"That's obvious." If he wanted me for a sounding board, I was willing. I had just learned from Iris how to do it. "So?"

"It has to be a strong reason," he went on, "not something trivial."

"I don't know about that, Warren. Wives have killed their husbands because they didn't squeeze the toothpaste from the bottom."

"In close relationships, yes. But Kassel wasn't close to any of our executives."

"They were all acquainted with him ten years ago."

"He wasn't killed ten years ago; he was killed now, for the speaker."

"How would killing him get anyone the speaker, Warren? Whether Kassel is alive or dead, the speaker belongs to Hamilcar Hi-Fi in a few days. Everything is in escrow; Kassel's death doesn't stop the transfer of title."

"Maybe the killer didn't know that, Dad."

"All of our execs went over the contract a dozen times. In case of death, the heirs or assigns get the initial money

149

and the royalties, but the company must get the speaker."

"Could the killer be an assignee of Kassel's?"

"If he is, he better not exercise that right. Palmieri would·have him in handcuffs before he finished talking. And then he'd get absolutely zero, guaranteed. A criminal may not benefit financially from his crime."

"Carter Hamilton is the biggest individual stockholder; he gets a quarter of the money we don't have to pay Kassel."

"Everything but the consulting fees has to go to Kassel's estate. I don't see Carter taking that kind of risk for five grand, taxable. And if that's what Carter wanted, why right now? He'd make just as much two weeks later, after the patent application was filed."

Warren was silent for a minute, then spoke again. "Glory. Carter was going to call it the HHF-10 and tell people that he and Borovic designed it."

"That wouldn't work, Warren. Kassel's name is still on the application, along with the assignment to Hamilcar. Everyone would know who the inventor really was."

"How about jealousy, Dad? Borovic has to be boiling that Kassel outdid him."

"I'm sure he is, inside. But how does killing Kassel change that?"

"Rollie is frantic to get to the show on time so he can make enough money to take care of his mother."

"So why didn't he kill Kassel two months ago, when it would do some good? And where he could grab the speaker and open it up?"

"George Sambur was convinced that Kassel was deliberately stretching out the testing. He hates cheats."

"The way I read George, he's keeping a file on Kassel, and will deduct the excess time from Kassel's royalties. I can't see George killing while he has the right to write the potential victim's checks."

Warren seemed to be grasping at straws. "Lou Russo,"

he said. "He's very excitable, always on edge. Kassel could have said the wrong thing to him at just the wrong time."

"And Lou exploded? Come on, Warren, this was not a crime of passion. It was calculated, cold."

"Fred Gorman has a lean and hungry look. Maybe instead of wanting to get the speaker sooner, he was trying to delay getting the speaker as a way to destroy the company and get rid of Carter Hamilton."

"So where does that leave Gorman? There aren't all that many jobs available for ex–vice presidents of a dead company."

Warren stood up. "There," he said, "that's exactly how I figured. Now do you see why I'm going crazy?"

"Me, too," I admitted. I cast about in my mind. All I could come up with was "Janie Zausmer?" Warren looked disgusted. "All right, all right," I said. "So maybe we were wrong. Maybe it *was* an outsider."

"Not possible, Dad. Why would an outsider kill Kassel in an anechoic chamber of a factory where there are dozens of people around who would recognize him as an outsider? And at the one time and place where he could not steal Kassel's speaker?"

I hadn't really thought so either, but what other choice was there? "Why, by the same reasoning, would an insider," I asked, "an exec, kill Kassel at the one place and time where he not only could *not* get the speaker—and even if he did get the speaker it would be like signing a confession—but he would be delaying the production of the speaker and jeopardizing his own income?"

"Exactly, Dad. So who had a motive? Nobody? Is one of our executives a homicidal maniac who gets a kick out of killing old men?"

"And does it once every ten years? In an anechoic chamber? No. What this means is that there is a motive that we haven't considered yet, which isn't money, sex, glory, jealousy, anger, fear, any of the usual ones. Maybe it's a combination of two of these, or more, in an odd mixture."

"Or maybe," Warren said, wearily, "it's one of these in an unusual form, which I haven't discovered yet. But I've thought of this, too. I've tried every permutation of motives I could think of for four solid hours, and nothing fits. I've never been so frustrated in my life." He looked ready to cry.

"Go to sleep, Warren," I said. "Relax and put the whole thing out of your mind. If it comes, it comes. If it doesn't . . . well, we'll still live."

Live? Yes, but Warren would have failed. I'd have to figure out how to take charge of the case again so that when we failed I would be the failure.

It wouldn't be the first time I'd failed. I could take it.

XXIV

I couldn't sleep, something was nagging me that much. Something one of them had done. Or said. Or let slip.

I went over everything in my mind, and everyone. I don't have a photographic memory, but in the building line you make deals; you can't write everything into a contract, so you get used to remembering the important details. That's easy. But the only way you can convince the other guy that your recollection is right when you remind him of what he promised, is to fill in the whole situation: the time, the place, the weather, who said what before and after, even the color of his shirt.

So that's what I was doing instead of sleeping. After a while it came to me. Gorman. He had said something about not being mad at Carter Hamilton anymore. But I couldn't remember the exact words. I had been too busy concentrating on his business disagreements with Carter. So I'd have to winkle it out of him.

I checked the clock. After two A.M. Good. He'd be mad as well as sleepy. The only question was where to probe. Doubtful it was money, so sex was it.

"Do you realize what time it is?" Gorman growled into the phone.

"Just a couple of questions," I said, "then you can go back to sleep. Were you and Carter roommates when you introduced him to Betsy Collins?"

"Of course we were, Baer. How else would he have met her?"

That was all I really needed, but just to round things out I asked, "Were you and Betsy engaged at the time?"

"Not formally, otherwise . . ." Then his mind must have snapped clear. "What are you getting at, Baer?"

"Betsy fell for Carter right away? Love at first sight?"

"Carter made sure everyone knew he would inherit millions. Betsy believed him. Even Carter believed it."

"So you've hated him ever since, Fred?"

"Come on, Baer, that was eleven years ago. I joined him in Hamilcar a year later."

"And spent all your time since sabotaging him, Fred. Killing Kassel was the final touch."

"You're grasping at straws, Baer." His voice was calm now, controlled. "Check the records if you want to see who saved Hamilcar from some of Carter's stupidities."

"Then why did you keep all this from me, Fred? That you've hated Carter for years over the girl."

"I didn't hide anything. Everyone who knows Carter knows the story; he tells it often enough. I was sore for a month, that's all. Then I realized how lucky I was. I could have been married and divorced from her by now if it wasn't for Carter. They deserve each other. Carter wasn't always a hippie, you know."

"But you did want to push Carter out and take control of the company."

"I'd do a much better job, and you know it. But what has that got to do with Kassel?"

"If Carter were blamed for the murder . . ."

"Baer, if I couldn't find ten easier ways to cut Carter's throat than by killing Kassel, I'd turn in my MBA and go into construction. And just in case you didn't know it, none of us liked Carter. So go and wake somebody else, now. Good night."

The phone was slammed down. So much for that. For

a moment I thought of calling Rollie Franklin and asking him if he was a member of the Jewish Defense League and Kassel had been a Nazi, a member of the German-American Bund, before the war. But that was even stupider than thinking that Gorman had held a grudge over a girl for eleven years and then got his revenge by killing a stranger he hadn't even met four months ago in the hope of framing Carter.

I decided not to mention this to Warren. The last thing I needed was to have him lose confidence in me as well as in himself. Maybe, even, I should turn in my detective badge and go back into construction. There, at least, I knew what I was doing.

XXV

All through our early breakfast, Warren wore a worried face. I wasn't pushing, but I couldn't just say nothing. So I said something. "Anything?"

"Maybe," he answered. "But I don't know what. I dreamed I had the solution, and I was completely satisfied. But when I woke up, I didn't remember a thing."

"The whole solution or just the motive?"

"I was concentrating on the motive, examining the information from every angle, so I imagine it was just the motive. But I'm sure that will lead to the whole solution. How did you do, Dad?"

"Marvelous. I can prove, beyond a reasonable doubt, that no one could have killed Kassel under these conditions."

"And I can prove logically that no one had anything to gain, or even to lose, that was worth killing Kassel for."

All of the good feelings he had yesterday seemed to have evaporated. I had to throw him something, no matter how foolish. "How about all six of them working together, in combination? Agatha Christie–style?"

He looked at me wanly. "You think I didn't try that? It was one of the first things I analyzed last night. Not just all six, but by twos and threes. There are fifteen different ways to combine two of them and twenty different ways to put three of them together. And they all stink. Can you imagine Carter Hamilton or Fred Gorman putting himself in a position to be blackmailed by Rollie Franklin? Or by George Sambur? Or John Borovic teaming up with Tony Russo?"

"But if they're in it together, the blackmailer would be cutting his own throat if he talked."

"The guy who turns state's evidence gets off easiest if he talks. No, it has to be a single killer." He paused a moment. "A single killer without a motive." Warren shook his head. "Maybe we ought to give up the whole idea, Dad; leave it to the police."

I couldn't let this happen. "No, Warren, we don't give up. We never walk away from a problem. The trouble is, we've been pushing too hard. For three days solid, we've been immersed in this case, every minute nothing but. We have to take a break. Listen, I'm going to go to the club, play a round, take out my frustrations on the ball. Why don't you go to the gym, take a workout, a little steam, a massage even. Don't think about motives, methods, business; just relax. Tomorrow, we start thinking about the case again. What do you say?"

"Might as well," he answered. I'll meet you for lunch in the Club Dining Room, say one o'clock."

I don't think I know how to relax yet. For that I have some evidence. I shot over 100, way over, on the *first* nine holes. The *last* nine was not that good. You wouldn't believe how many balls I used up; a club record, but who needs records like that? A whirlpool and a hot shower didn't help, and the masseur told me he had never felt me so tense, that a massage wouldn't help, what I needed was a concrete breaker.

I'm not a drinker, ask anybody, but when I sat down to lunch, where Warren was already waiting for me, I ordered a double-double-extra-very-dry martini, no olives, they take up too much room, and I didn't sip it slowly. I started with a fresh fruit cup, laced with plenty of Kirsch, but plenty I told Clarence, my regular waiter, who understands these things. Then black bean soup, easy on the soup, heavy on the sherry; breast of Long Island duckling au calvados, lots and lots of gravy, no flaming, ruins the effect of the gravy, and no vegetables; then Irish coffee, not too stingy on the Irish, with, on the side, baba au rhum in a big bowl, so there'd be enough room for the basic flavoring to come through, with the baba floating, you understand, not just soaked, but *floating,* to be called Floating Rhum au Baba à la Baer. This, I had made my mind up, was going to be a very relaxing meal.

I urged Warren to follow my lead, but he assured me that breathing at the same table with me would be relaxing enough, and that I should give notes to some of the other diners to take home to their wives.

It worked, too. I never felt so relaxed in my life. It's true, you are what you eat; absolutely true. By the time of the duckling, everything was beautiful, clear, and beautifully clear. Clearly beautiful. But I wanted to make sure, so after my coffee and cake, I sipped, slowly, like a gentleman, a double Armagnac. Then I asked Warren to drive me to my old pal, good old Sergeant Ben Palmieri, who I was going to do a big favor to.

Palmieri didn't believe me at first, but I swore to him, on my honor as an engineer, that I had the case solved. Not actually everything, but how it was done. Perfectly, absolutely, beautifully, crystal clear. All he had to do was assemble all the suspects in Hamilton's office and watch their faces as I artfully revealed how the murder was done, that's all he had to do—was that too much to ask?—which was absolutely positively guaranteed to get him, Palmieri, a gold star, and the guy who looked guilty was the guilty guy, right? Obviously.

No, there was no way I was going to tell him now, it would spoil the surprise. The whole point was to shock the killer, who thought he was so smart but he hadn't reckoned on Edward Baer, ha, ha, who would show him what's what. Absolutely, definitely, guaranteed foolproof. Of course I was sober; only had one drink, not counting the aperitif, and that was after a full meal, ask Warren, but if it made him feel better, I would take a cold shower and drink lots of coffee.

Five o'clock would be perfect, they'd all be tired and nervous, but Palmieri, good old Ben, would have to tell them *right now,* so the killer would have plenty of time to get even more nervous. No, I didn't know who did it; that was a mere detail, it could have been any one of the six. I just knew how, but it was guaranteed, definitely, positively, one hundred percent one of those six. Bring a stenographer and a couple of big cops in case the killer got nasty.

The last thing I remember was Warren promising Palmieri that he would deliver me at five, sober. And that I was perfectly reliable and never made promises I couldn't keep. Sober? Absolute nonsense. Could I have figured it all out if I was not absolutely, perfectly, completely, in full command of my senses? All of them? Didn't I prove that if you're taking a relaxing meal, you always start with fresh fruit salad?

Fresh fruit salad is very healthy, full of fiber.

Ask anybody.

XXVI

Warren had brought along Doris Starr, my secretary, to take notes. Good thinking, Warren.

The six suspects made a united front, sitting in a line along the wall behind Carter Hamilton's desk. Warren and I confronted them about ten feet in front of the desk. Palmieri sat in the back corner at my left, next to the police secretary. Doris was in the back right corner. The two policemen were standing flanking the door. Big ones. Good.

"Gentlemen," I said, trying not to move my head too much, "we are gathered here together for me to reveal a mystery that has been puzzling you, five of you at least, for several days, and to ask you to analyze, with your finely trained technical minds, the solution that it has been incumbent upon me to reveal." I don't usually talk this way, but I wanted to impress the gravity of the situation on them and to show Sergeant Palmieri how beneficial relaxation is.

"Get to the point, Ed," Carter said. "It's late, and we're all tired."

"You all, except the killer, of course, have been trying to figure out how Walter Kassel was killed in the anechoic chamber where he could not be approached without his knowing it at once, where Kassel would have seen the killer had he been there in advance, and where there was

160

no room to get between Kassel and the test rig. Any one of you could have entered or left the airlock relatively safely, at either level, and each of you, except for Carter, was seen near an airlock within a few minutes of the murder, so a careful check of the timetables would prove nothing."

"Ed," Carter said wearily, "none of us did it. We had no reason. Kassel brought us the speaker that saved our company. He may have been obnoxious as a person, but it was because of his invitation that your group invested the money we needed. Don't try to pin the crime on any of us."

"When I'm finished, Carter, you'll see that it had to be one of you. And where were you, Carter, when Kassel was killed?"

"In my office."

"Can you prove it? Doesn't your office have a side door leading directly into a basement stair?"

"I don't have to prove anything," he said coolly. "And you better watch what you say in front of the police. There's a lot at stake here. For all of us."

I decided to continue my explanation, staring straight at Carter as I spoke, looking for signs of guilt. Of all the executives, he would be the easiest to replace; Fred Gorman could step into his shoes on one minute's notice. "What kept me," I said, "and everyone else, from seeing the solution, was the assumption that the killing was done shortly after lunch four days ago. Well, the actual stabbing was, but the murder was started at least a week before, maybe even longer. You know those hanging ladders in the warehouse area? The ones with the hooks on the end that hang from the top shelf?"

"Yeah," said Tony Russo, "I gave you three of them the other day to get on the top of the chamber."

"Exactly. They're light, about a foot wide and twelve feet long. Well, the killer moved one of them to the end of the aisle near the door of the lower airlock one day, when no one was watching. The light is dim in the aisles between the stacks of speakers, and the workmen never notice an executive walking around. It took only a few seconds, and if he were seen, the killer could have used the ladder to check a top shelf."

"What's wrong with moving a ladder?" George Sambur asked. "I do it myself on occasion, to spot-check inventory. If you think that just because my fingerprints are on a ladder that—"

"Relax, George, I'm not saying who, only how. Anyway, a day or two later, maybe three, at night after the workmen went home, the killer put this ladder into the lower airlock. Again, it took only a few seconds."

"Now wait, Ed," Fred Gorman said, "these airlocks are only five feet square and the ladder is twelve feet long. You can't even open both the inner and the outer airlock doors at the same time, that's how small it is."

"Vertically," John Borovic said. "The airlocks are the same height as the chamber sections. Fifteen feet for the lower one, twenty feet for the upper one. The ladder could be stood up easily."

"Then one or two nights later," I continued, "the killer put the ladder in the chamber, laying it on top of the cylinders that make up the floor of the lower section. He placed it about five feet from the test jig above in the upper section. Kassel would not see the ladder, fifteen feet below the netting, since the lights he brought in were focused on the test jig. The killer then sneaked out, opening the airlock door a crack to make sure no one was watching. The whole thing took one minute."

"Anybody could have done that," Rollie Franklin pointed out. "Even you, Ed, if you come down to it. And how does that help? Kassel was killed on the upper level, not the lower. You can't get through the rope netting without cutting it."

"True, Rollie," I answered, "but Kassel was killed from the lower level. Here's how. He bolted the speaker to the test rig—"

"Wait," Warren shouted, then looked embarrassed. "I'm sorry to interrupt, Dad, but we don't know that, we just assumed it. We forgot to ask Janie Zausmer that question." He turned to Palmieri. "Please, Sergeant, tell me, was Kassel's speaker on the test rack or not?"

Palmieri looked confused and stubborn at the same time. "I don't know if I should tell you that," he finally said.

"We can always ask Mrs. Zausmer," Warren reminded him gently.

"Yeah, I guess you can. All right, the speaker was on the test rack."

"Was it bolted on?" Warren pressed. "Were the nuts tight? Were the wires hooked up, ready for testing?"

"Look, Mr. Baer," Palmieri said. "You got to understand. The right way, normal police procedure, is not to tell everything. That way, if somebody confesses, we can check what he says against the facts and we know if he's telling the truth or not."

"Please, Sergeant," Warren begged, "we gave you information we found out. Freely. We didn't ask anything in return. But you still have plenty of secrets, the type of knife, other things like that. I promise you, I swear, if you give me, tell me, that the speaker was fully connected, I'll give you the name of the killer."

"Just from that?"

"Not just from that, Sergeant. But I can see what my father is getting at, and when I put it together with what I've just figured out, I'll know who killed Kassel."

"Knowing isn't enough, Mr. Baer. I need evidence to make a case that the D.A. can take to the grand jury."

"Evidence? Yes, I'll give you evidence."

Palmieri sat quietly for a full minute, his face not moving. When he spoke, his tone was formal. "I could get a reprimand for this, but I'll take a chance on you. Okay, the speaker was on the test rack, the bolts were tight, wrench tight, and the wires were hooked up, all ready for the testing."

Warren let his breath out, "Thank you, Sergeant." We all let our breaths out, although I, for sure, didn't know what Warren saw. "Okay, Dad," Warren said, "keep going. You're absolutely right in your reconstruction."

Well, that was a relief to know; now that the cold shower and the coffee were taking effect, I wasn't as absolutely sure as I had been before. "Okay." I faced the line of suspects with renewed confidence. "Kassel finishes hooking up the speaker. Total time from when he entered the airlock, a few minutes. Now we switch to the killer. As soon as he knew Kassel was definitely going to enter the airlock, remember, all you guys were watching, he went at once to the lower airlock. It was near the end of lunchtime, not too many people around. When the coast was clear he slipped into the lower chamber—"

"It was dark in there," Palmieri said. "How did he walk on the cylinders?"

"He used a tiny flashlight, a penlight, to locate the intersections of the cylinders so he could place his feet on them, and walked to where the ladder was that he had left there before. To make the walking easier, he wore sneakers," all eyes turned to Carter Hamilton, "or crepe-rubber-soled shoes." Their eyes turned away, each of the six looking at the others, clearly trying to remember who wore what that day.

"Okay," I continued, "the killer is waiting down below, watching Kassel. As soon as Kassel finished hooking up the speakers, the killer lifted the ladder. Kassel couldn't see him, the lights were shining on the test rig and the killer was behind Kassel. The killer hooked the ladder onto the rope netting about five feet behind Kassel and put all his weight suddenly on the ladder, actually starting to climb the ladder, very fast. Kassel fell over backward, to the low spot on the netting, as did the light tripod. The killer reached in his left hand through the net, pushed the knife into Kassel's heart, and climbed down the ladder. Unhooking the ladder, he carried it to the airlock, and left as soon as the coast was clear. I don't know if he hung the ladder back on its shelf right away or later, after the body was discovered but before the police came, but that doesn't matter."

There was dead silence. Palmieri broke it, heavily. "Why did he reach around to stab Kassel in the front with his left hand? Why didn't he just stab Kassel in the back with his right hand? Are you saying the killer was left-handed?" All eyes turned to Fred Gorman.

"Not necessarily," I said. "Kassel was stabbed in the front rather than in the back so the blood wouldn't drip down on the killer. Which is additional proof that it was done from below. And he used his left hand because otherwise he would have had to reach too far around Kassel to stab him in the heart."

"I'll buy that, Mr. Baer," Palmieri said. "But what have I got?"

"Yes," Carter Hamilton said, "that's an ingenious explanation, but there is absolutely no evidence that one of us did it. What you described could have been done by anyone in the plant at the time."

"But the killer would also have to have been in the plant in the previous week," I pointed out. "Which leaves out a lot of people."

"The first part, the preparation," said Gorman, "could have been done by one person and the actual killing by another."

"True," I admitted. "Very unlikely, but possible. But will you geniuses see if you can find any flaws in what I said? Or come up with another way, no matter how crazy, to explain the facts in the case?"

Again dead silence, not even heavy breathing. I could have been in the anechoic chamber, for all I knew. Make that the "dead room"; one of these guys would hang for murder some day.

"Why was it done in this complicated way?" Palmieri asked.

"For the same reason I don't know *who* did it," I replied, "even though I know *how* it was done. The killer was sure that if the police didn't know how it was done, they'd never be able to figure out who did it."

"That ain't necessarily so," Palmieri said. "Even before you explained how the crime was perpetrated, I knew that one of these six guys had to have done it. Hell, I knew that five minutes after I stepped into the place."

"Sure," I said, "intuition. But you didn't know which one, and there's no way you could have known that without knowing how the murder was committed. Even Warren didn't know who until I explained the how. So that's why the killer went to all this trouble, to give himself another layer of protection. He knew that the police would figure it had to be one of the executives and he wanted to make sure they'd never be able to figure out it was him."

"It is also possible," George Sambur said, his pudgy face covered with sweat, "that the killer didn't want any of his colleagues accused of the crime, either. Notice that there were no clues pointing directly to me—that is, to any of us." He looked around nervously.

"I prefer my version," I said. "I don't have any faith in the kindness of murderers." I stared at each one of the executives in turn. They stirred uncomfortably. Rollie Franklin was smoothing his moustache over and over again. Tony Russo's face was red; I could imagine what was going on inside his stomach. Carter Hamilton had his lips pressed together, staring daggers at me. John Borovic was holding his hands clasped tightly together, as though to keep from smashing my face. Only Fred Gorman looked cool.

I let them stew, motioning Warren to wait. Five full minutes I let them sweat; there's nothing like a man's own imagination to put pressure on him. And I watched carefully. Trouble was, they all looked guilty. Finally, it was enough. Nothing more to gain by waiting, no one was going to confess.

"Okay," I said, "you had your chance. Now Warren is going to tell who did it."

XXVII

Warren stood up, leaning on the back of his chair, like the professor he really was at heart. "If Kassel was killed for money," he said, "or love, hate, revenge, any of the usual motives, why not in his room? Or in the street? You want to know the safest way to kill someone? Hit him with your car. Claim you lost control. Or you could slug him some night when he was coming home from the factory where he did his off-the-books work, and no one would ever know. You could even steal his speaker, very easily, except that if you tried to sell it, or claim it as your own, the police would know you were the killer.

"Yet," Warren continued, "there is no doubt that Kassel was killed because of the speaker. What else was there to kill him for? But why did he have to be killed in the anechoic chamber? That's the crux of the puzzle. Let me go back a bit." Warren paused, as if to find the correct words. "My first assumption was that someone was trying to steal Kassel's speaker, or rather, the secret of the Kassel speaker. And it was true that we all wanted to expose what was inside it, the sooner the better; we were all angry with Kassel for being such a stubborn, suspicious old man, worrying that someone would steal his invention, making us wait until the patent application was filed.

"But there were things that did not fit," Warren went on. "Kassel never told anyone what the invention that was stolen from him years ago was. Have you ever spoken to an inventor who wouldn't describe, for hours, how General Motors or General Electric or some big company is making billions from something he thought of first? Kassel didn't. Have you ever known an inventor or designer—ask Mr. Slowicki—who was in such a hurry to get the latest drawings or text of a patent application that he couldn't wait for the mail but came to the patent attorney's office to pick them up, and yet didn't read the papers right away? Walter Kassel didn't. He quietly took the papers and left. Without discussion or comment. He wanted speed all right, he was back in one or two days with the typed text changes and the neat drawing revisions, but he never discussed them with Mr. Slowicki.

"Then there was another strange thing. Kassel worked nights for two employers. One we traced down easily. The other? No one knew anything about him. My father offered a reward to one of the men who employed Kassel to find out who Kassel's other employer was. That man never called to collect. Why couldn't he find out who Kassel's other employer was? Could Kassel have been working at night in a place where no other machinist ever worked? Or in a place that was not a machine shop?"

Warren looked at the six suspects; they were paying close attention. "Another question," he said. "Where did Kassel work on the patent application? There was no typewriter in his room, no drafting table. Maybe he used the typewriter and the drafting equipment in the machine shop he worked in occasionally. But he couldn't count on its being available when he wanted it; and he did bring the corrections back to his attorney in one or two days. And his employer was not dissatisfied with his production. So where and when did he make the drawings and the text, the beautiful professional drawings and the accurate text?"

I was beginning to get the picture, so I moved my chair a little, sort of casually, so that I could dive between Warren and whoever of the six it happened to be, in a hurry.

Warren kept lecturing, in that calm, professorial voice. "It's not impossible for an attic inventor to invent a novel device; it's rare these days but it has been done. But usually it's done by someone interested in the field, deep into some hobby. What was Kassel's hobby? According to his landlady, watching television. Hardly the type to invent a new principle of sound reproduction. And the attic inventor usually starts with a crude model and tests it and refines it out of love and pride, far beyond what is required for reduction to practice. I'm sure Kassel made the loudspeaker, he was a good machinist. But where did he test it? With what equipment? If he tested it strictly by ear, which is crazy since the older you get the less able you are to hear high frequencies, which records did he use? There were no audiophile quality records in his room; there were no records at all. There wasn't even a record player. Wouldn't you all agree that this was highly unusual?" The execs shifted uneasily in their seats.

"Then there was Kassel's secrecy," Warren went on. "Understandable, yes, but carried to such extremes? No one but Kassel could test the speaker, or even touch it. Not even after all the papers were signed. No description of the operating principle. If it were anything but a speaker, where the results are immediately clear and externally testable, Kassel would have been thrown out. So why didn't Kassel want to describe anything, reveal anything, explain anything?"

Warren paused as if waiting for a response from his class. Just squirming. Warren started lecturing again. "Other clues. Why was Kassel so insistent on getting his four-hundred-dollar-a-week consulting fee? And why did the testing take so long? Wouldn't a normal inventor have tried to complete the tests quickly, to get his big first payment and to see his brainchild in production? Kassel acted as though the only real money was the consulting fee; the front-end money was less real. And what about his paranoid insistence on secrecy? The papers were escrowed with his own attorney. Why was it so important that the patent application, naming Kassel as the inventor, be filed before any disclosure?"

Warren stared at each executive in turn. Each met Warren's eyes, but very uncomfortably, it seemed to me. "This leads to other questions," Warren continued. "Why did Kassel choose this company? And why did he do it at exactly the time he did? True, he had had some very slight contact with Hamilcar ten years ago, but didn't Nassau Model ever do business with any other speaker company? And why was Kassel killed just before the Las Vegas show? What was there that made his death necessary at the worst possible time for Hamilcar Hi-Fi? Was it the Vegas show that was the deadline, or something else? What else was there at that time, other than the filing of the patent application?"

There was dead silence for a minute. Warren let the class think before he spoke again. I could see the gears turning in their heads; they were, after all, intelligent executives and engineers. "If Kassel was killed," Warren said, "to delay the filing of the patent, it didn't work, did it? Given Kassel's stalling, the filing may even have been speeded up a day or two *because* Kassel was killed. On the other hand, if Kassel was killed to speed up the filing, then why wasn't he killed a month ago? Or two months ago?"

Warren paused dramatically. Every eye was on Warren; everyone was sweating, even me. I could sense the pattern, almost, but it was not quite there. This time Warren spoke very quietly, but we all heard him clearly. "The most important clue was that Kassel was killed in the dead room. Of all places, the dead room. If the killer wanted the speaker design, why pick the one place where it was certain that the speaker would be out of reach for a day or two, at least? And would then have to be opened in front of all the executives?"

Palmieri was leaning forward, concentrating hard. I

could see Carter looking at Palmieri instead of Warren. "So," Warren said, "when Sergeant Palmieri told me the speaker was bolted to the frame before Kassel was killed, I had the final proof. If the killer wanted to know what was inside the speaker, the time to kill Kassel was when he was carrying the light tripod and the speaker; then Kassel was in the easiest position to be thrown off balance. The speaker would have fallen to the netting without damage. Two slashes of a knife and the speaker would be in the killer's hands. He could open it in the chamber or in the airlock. Or take it home for detailed study, hidden in an HHF-1 carton. So why didn't the killer murder Kassel then? Why did he wait until the speaker was bolted to the stand?"

Warren looked around, as if for a show of hands from his students. No hands, not even mine. "Because," Warren said triumphantly, "because the killer didn't need to know what was inside the speaker. He *already* knew. He *wanted* the speaker opened in front of all the other executives. And he *wanted* the speaker ready for testing, to speed up the process leading to the production model."

The room might as well have been an anechoic chamber, it was that quiet. The six suspects stared straight ahead, carefully not looking at one another. Palmieri was sitting up alertly, his holster flap unbuttoned. I turned around. The two policemen at the door were casually resting their hands on their gun butts.

"So we have a peculiar situation. The killer wants the speaker tested and in production. but he doesn't want to wait one more day for Kassel to complete the tests. He doesn't want to know what's inside the speaker enclosure, but he wants the speaker on the test rig, ready for completion of the tests. He's in a hurry, but he doesn't mind the time the chamber is closed during the inevitable investigation. Why? Because he needed Kassel dead right at that time. Why? What was his motive?"

That's what I wanted to know. Why. And who. Teachers can be very irritating at times.

"It's clear," Warren said, "that not only was Kassel in no danger of having his invention stolen, Kassel himself was the thief. He had stolen the speaker from someone else. But how could this be? Kassel was not an engineer, not educated, not even an audiophile. He wouldn't know a good speaker from a jukebox. So who told him the speaker was great, that it derived from a new principle? Who gave him the drawings and the text, made the corrections and revisions on the papers that Kassel brought him from Slowicki's office? Who gave Kassel the money, in cash, to pay for the patent draftsman, the filing fee, Slowicki's out-of-pocket expenses? Who else, but the real inventor of the speaker?"

There was an almost imperceptible edging away of the others from Carter Hamilton and John Borovic. Palmieri looked from one of the designers to the other. Warren's calm voice went on, the philosophy professor hammering home, with unassailable logic, the nails in the coffin. Given the facts, absolute certainties, no way to refute them, all that could be done was to await the inevitable.

"But why would the inventor of the speaker choose to give all this to Walter Kassel? Because he knew Kassel slightly from ten years ago, when Kassel worked for Nassau Model. Because Kassel was an expert machinist and would do good work. Because Kassel was poor and, for a few dollars, would do whatever his master ordered. Because Walter Kassel was old and had lost all ambition, was just trying to get along. Because Walter Kassel was honest, and not very intelligent; he would never think of double-crossing his master. Or, even if he did, he would not know how.

"But why," Warren asked, "why would the inventor of the speaker not patent the device himself? Why use Kassel at all? There was a good reason to use Kassel to make the model, the prototype, but should it not have been done under a confidential-disclosure agreement? Why let Kassel apply for a patent under his own name?" Warren paused again. Maybe it was unconscious, but it sure was dramatic. "Simple. Because the inventor couldn't patent it under his own name. Because the inventor was an officer, a stockholder, and an employee of Hamilcar Hi-Fi, who had signed a typical designer's agreement with the company that anything he invented or designed belonged to the company, not only now but for five years after he left the company. There was no way for the inventor to gain from this all by himself. He would have to share the fruits of his genius with five other people. *His* brilliance, *his* invention, and he would get only a tiny part of the return.

"There are only two people in this company who are speaker designers," Warren's voice turned hard, accusing. "Carter Hamilton and John Borovic. Two years ago, when this invention was first conceived, Carter Hamilton owned fifty percent of the company. The company was getting into financial difficulties. Is it possible that Carter, in order to get one hundred percent of the gains from his invention rather than fifty percent, would destroy his own company? That he would allow Nassau Venture Capital to come into the picture at all, reducing his equity to twenty-five percent? Or even less since, surely, he promised Kassel a share of the profits? If you add to this the fact that Kassel came to Hamilcar exactly on the day when one person was out of town—and how would Kassel know that, unless—the answer is clear. The inventor of the super-speaker was John Borovic."

XXVIII

John looked coolly at Warren. "That's an interesting line of guesswork and conjecture, Warren. I feel honored that you think I'm capable of inventing the Kassel speaker. But your lengthy speech in front of my colleagues and the police has caused me damage. If you have no proof, and you can't have since all of this is lies, it's going to cost you plenty. Unless you want to retract and apologize right now. I'm not looking to cause any trouble."

I didn't say a word. This was Warren's ball game.

Warren didn't even blink. I was proud of him. But come to think of it, he must have had a much harder time defending his dissertation. I felt he would *schlomm* Borovic.

"I see no need to apologize, Mr. Borovic, and I'm sorry you're threatening me with legal action. All I did was point out that you were the inventor of the Borovic speaker, a brilliant piece of work. I *do* accuse you of being the mysterious voice that used to call Kassel at night and that would not identify itself, but again, that's no crime."

"Are you saying that he didn't kill Kassel," Palmieri asked, "the way your father described?"

"I didn't say that either, Sergeant. But let me lay my groundwork first. Simple Aristotelian logic, but, for my purpose, it will do admirably. For example, why did Borovic use Kassel as a front? Simple. He wanted one hundred percent, not ten percent. How was he to prevent

Kassel from cheating him? He had Kassel sign legal papers that Borovic was the inventor and owned all rights, and that Kassel was Borovic's agent and had no rights to the invention. If Kassel tried to sell the invention anywhere, Borovic could pull the string, and he'd be no worse off than before. He'd get, at least, his ten percent.

"So Borovic conceived a plan. Hamilcar was doing badly; all it needed was one final push to put it out of business. I don't know who first came up with the idea for the HHF-2, but it's highly probable that Borovic, if not the originator of the idea, was one of its strongest advocates."

The other five executives looked at one another. There were small nods, general agreement. "What if I was?" Borovic said. "There was need for a small, cheap speaker."

"Sure there was," Rollie Franklin said through gritted teeth. "But not for that piece of crap."

"Exactly," Warren agreed. "It is just not conceivable that the man who perfected the HHF-1 could produce the HHF-2, other than deliberately."

"What about the 1A?" Borovic said, desperately. "That was pure genius."

"It was," Warren said, "and everyone recognizes how good you are. But when it came, it was too little and too late. It wasn't enough even to persuade my father to invest in Hamilcar. You were trying to destroy the company."

"Why would I do that?" Borovic cried. "It was my company, too."

"Because six months later you would have been the majority stockholder of the Borovic Super-Speaker Company, having acquired the rights to the super-speaker from Kassel as per your agreement, and making millions. People would remember the 1A and forget the 2, which you could always claim was messed up by Carter Hamilton, the proof being the new super Borovic speaker.

"But Kassel fooled you. Either from something you

said, or Slowicki said, or just native shrewdness, Kassel figured out the one place he could go where you could not use the quitclaim on him: Hamilcar Hi-Fi. He carefully picked a time when you were away, and the person who would be most receptive, Rollie Franklin, and from that moment on, you were no longer master."

"Wait," Palmieri broke in. "Why didn't Borovic, at that time, tell the truth? Why didn't he just tell everybody that he was the real inventor of the speaker? I'm sure he could have proved it easily."

"Of course he could," Warren answered. "But if he admitted he was the real inventor, he was also admitting that he had broken his contract with Hamilcar. He would not only lose his rights to the invention, he could also have been thrown out of Hamilcar and even lost his ten percent. Or have it tied up in litigation for years; equally bad, from his point of view."

Borovic stood up, steaming. "All this is a crock of lies. You don't have a bit of proof. You don't even have a consistent story. Even if everything you said was true, why should I kill Kassel? What did I have to gain by it? Nothing!"

"Yes, that's the crux of the matter, Mr. Borovic, the motive," Warren said patiently. "Sit down and I'll explain. Or leave, if you wish, and I'll explain to Sergeant Palmieri without you. Wouldn't you prefer to hear what I have to say?"

Borovic sat down, glowering. I shifted my chair again, slightly, to be more between Borovic and Warren. An ordinary business precaution.

"Once Kassel came to Hamilcar," Warren said, "and claimed the speaker was his, with his name on the patent application as inventor, all of Borovic's plans were shattered. The most he could get out of this was to retain his stock ownership. Even then, he was still at Kassel's mercy. If Kassel ever told Hamilton or my father the truth, Borovic would be out and, in addition, would be sued for everything that Kassel had been given. Borovic would end up a pauper. But if Kassel died before the patent application was filed, or before the speaker was examined, things would be different. Not only would Borovic be freed of the threat of Kassel's blackmail, not only would Borovic get his share, no matter how small, of what Kassel would have been paid, but one other thing would have happened, something of major importance to all designers, all creators, all inventors. Borovic would have been recognized as the inventor of the greatest speaker of all time, the discoverer of a new principle of sound reproduction. Aside from the honor and the glory, there could be a tremendous financial gain. Borovic could threaten to leave Hamilcar and go with another company, or even get financing to start his own company, just on the strength of having created this design. He would, of course, lose everything he had in Hamilcar, but it might be worth it. Wouldn't you back a design genius of that caliber, Dad?''

"In spades, Warren. But how would he prove this without showing the papers that Kassel signed? We could take all his marbles for that.''

"Simple, Dad. Kassel had to be killed, first of all, so he couldn't talk. Second, Kassel had to be killed before the patent application was filed, I'll tell you why in a minute. I'm sure that Borovic wanted to kill Kassel weeks ago, but the circumstances weren't right until the day of the final test. Or, more likely, Borovic *had* to kill Kassel then, because there was no time left.

"Here's the scenario. Kassel is dead, and the speaker is opened carefully, by Borovic, in front of everybody, including Carter and Tony; no need to tell Slowicki. John pokes around and says, 'Wait a minute, this looks familiar.' He gets his bound idea notebook from his office, leafs through it, and lo! he finds some sketches showing the basic concepts and a note that he gave copies to Sam Moscow of Nassau Model just before Sam died, for evaluation of model costs. 'Hey,' says John, 'Sam must have given these to Kassel before he died. That bastard stole my idea.' Now John wouldn't have owned the whole patent, but he surely would have gotten a big bonus. Right, Dad?"

I nodded. "At least a quarter of what we would have given Kassel." Carter nodded, too.

"And Borovic would have gotten all the credit," Warren continued. "John's name would have gone on the patent application even though it was assigned to Hamilcar. The speaker would have been called the Borovic Super, and John could have written his own ticket after that. How's that for a motive, Dad?"

"Great." I turned to Borovic. "What do you have to say to that, you bastard?"

"Nothing." He smiled calmly. "This is all conjecture."

"Maybe it is," I spoke up, it was time, "but it all fits, now that Warren has fingered you. The hanging ladder that was the key to killing Kassel in the dead room. It's under twelve feet long and the netting is fifteen feet above the top of the basement sound cylinders. No matter how hard the killer yanked the netting down, the bottom rung of the ladder had to be almost three feet up. A short guy couldn't have gotten his foot on that bottom rung very easily, or climbed up fast enough to kill Kassel before he rolled away after falling over. Rollie and Sambur are not in the best shape for a fast climb. Maybe Carter has the agility, but he's pretty light; his weight wouldn't pull the netting down enough. Russo is heavy and strong, but he's so short he'd have to lift his foot waist high to get it near the rung. With his belly, forget it. Fred Gorman is tall, but he's skinny and not as strong as you are, John. So it has to be you."

"Doesn't mean a thing," Borovic said confidently.

"Something else does," I said. "Your feet. They're so big they could act as snowshoes. You could walk on the tops of the cylinders easier than anyone else."

"You're still shooting blanks, Ed," Borovic said. "This is no proof of anything. Ask Sergeant Palmieri."

The sergeant hadn't moved from his chair. He nodded to one of his men. "Go find the notebook, the one he writes his ideas in, in Borovic's office." The man left.

"Without a search warrant, Sergeant?" Borovic grinned. "That's the best way to make sure it can't be used in court."

"Don't teach me my business, son," Palmieri said. "I declare this whole building the scene of the crime and I can search anywhere I want in it."

Just for good luck, I spoke up. "Carter, would you, as president of Hamilcar, allow Sergeant Palmieri to search any part of the premises and to take possession of anything he finds there to be used as evidence?"

Carter smiled viciously. "You have my permission to do just that, Sergeant."

Palmieri turned to the second officer, who snapped to attention. Palmieri put one fist against his ear and another against his mouth, then nodded at Borovic. The officer nodded and left the office quickly. "You told me," Palmieri said to Borovic, "that you keep another notebook at home on your bedside for new ideas. I have a feeling that there may be some evidence in there the D.A. can use."

"You can't search my house without a warrant." Borovic sounded panicky.

"I wouldn't think of it, sir," Palmieri answered. "But where there is a clear presumption that evidence of a crime exists, and that evidence is in danger of being destroyed, there is such a thing as a phone warrant. You want to try to beat me to your house, sir? That would be interesting to the D.A. too, especially if you were caught trying to destroy that notebook."

I suddenly realized something. "Sergeant Palmieri," I said. "When you're searching his house, pick up his typewriter." I was waiting for it, and I saw Borovic's face twitch. Now I was sure, so I went on. "Because when Borovic typed the patent information, and the responses to the Patent Office actions, he didn't know he was going to kill Kassel. Compare the typescript with that on the patent papers Slowicki got from Kassel. Guaranteed they'll match."

"He had three days to get rid of the machine," Palmieri said resignedly.

"I'll bet he didn't," I said. "He couldn't do anything to call attention to himself, and he was absolutely positive no one could figure out how he killed Kassel, much less who did it."

Then I realized we had another clue, one nobody had thought of. "There's got to be something else in Borovic's house," I told Palmieri. "The detail drawings of the speaker."

Borovic really jumped at this. Palmieri looked puzzled. "When you tell a machinist what to make," I explained, "you don't say it. You make detailed drawings, to scale, with manufacturing tolerances shown. Borovic had to give prints of these drawings to Kassel to make the prototype speaker."

"We didn't find any drawings in Kassel's room," Palmieri said, "and we made a thorough search."

"Of course not," I said. "Borovic took each drawing back as soon as the part was finished."

"It would have been good to have them," Palmieri sighed, "but he probably burned the drawings a month ago."

"No, he didn't," I told him. "He needed the drawings to make the model speakers for the show. That's why he wasn't worried about the testing delays. And also why he didn't want any of his partners accused of murder. He needed them all to pitch in to produce the speaker in a hurry."

"Wouldn't they have been suspicious," Palmieri asked, "if he had the drawings?"

"He would have delivered them one at a time, claiming he was working night and day to push them out."

Just then the second officer came back. Palmieri told him to take the typewriter, too, as evidence, and any engineering drawings he found as well.

Borovic's eyes were snapping from Palmieri to me and back again. "You're framing me!" Borovic shouted. "You're all jealous. You can't prove a thing."

"I think," Warren said, "that Kassel's landlady, Mrs. Dolan, might recognize your voice."

"On the phone?" Borovic sneered. "You're kidding."

"No one mentioned a phone, sir," Palmieri said. "Why did you?"

"Just a wild guess. It doesn't mean a thing. You won't find any fingerprints on the knife."

"Now how would you know that, sir?" Palmieri asked. "Did you dispose of the gloves already? No matter. I'll bet you bought that knife within the past few weeks within a five-mile radius of here or your home. We'll find out where; we're very patient and very good at things like that, and we'll see if the clerk remembers you."

"I'll fight you. I'll get the best lawyer; the company will have to pay for it. Everything I did was for the good of the company."

This was the time for Ed Baer. Warren had done fine, but there are some things he doesn't know how to do yet. Someday he would, from watching me operate, but this was my play now.

"Borovic," I said, "you are no longer with the company, Carter has just fired you. Right, Carter?" Carter gave a firm "Yes."

"You broke your contract," I went on. "Not by accident, but in bad faith. Your salary stops as of this moment and the company and I and all the other stockholders will sue you personally for the money we paid Kassel, for the other costs, for the damages, for the delays, for the moral turpitude that reflects on the company name, for the overtime that Tony has to put in to make the Las Vegas show on time, and for anything else I can think of. By the time I'm finished with you I'll tie up all your assets and you'll have to borrow a quarter to call the public defender. I'll strip you so naked your wife and kids will have to go on welfare. You won't have enough assets to get out on bail even. You want to tangle with me? I'm ready."

Warren looked at me in amazement. He had never seen me really angry, in action, before. But there are things you learn in the construction business, things you *have* to learn just to stay alive, that they don't teach you in school. Borovic pulled back in his chair, away from me, rigid with fear.

"But," I said, "I'll offer you one out, one time. You take it now, because if you even stop to think it over, I walk out of here and go to work on you, and believe me, when I'm finished with you, there'll be nothing left."

"Sergeant," I turned to Palmieri, "I understand that, with the kind of careful planning that went into this murder, the planning alone can be used by the prosecutor as evidence of premeditation."

"That is often the case, sir," Palmieri said guardedly.

"It is my understanding," I continued, "that if a person is convicted of first-degree murder, he can be sentenced to twenty-five-to-life. Isn't that so, Sergeant?"

"It can happen, sir."

"And that many people so sentenced are sent to Attica?"

"I'm not sure of the exact percentage, sir, but it is a sizable number."

"I hear that Attica is not a very pleasant place, Sergeant."

"I have never been there myself, but that's what I've been told, sir."

"What happens to nice-looking young white men who get sent to Attica?"

"The prison officials do not discriminate against them, sir, I am sure."

"That's not what I meant, Sergeant, but I realize that there are limits to what you can say. Tell me, does the D.A. take your recommendations?"

"On occasion he has, sir. Not always."

"Would it not save the police department time and energy, and the taxpayers a good deal of money, if an accused person were to plead guilty to a lesser charge, such as manslaughter?"

"That is probably true, sir, but it's not up to me."

"The corporative perpetrator who pleaded guilty to manslaughter, isn't it likely he'd draw five-to-fifteen in Elmira?"

"There is a good possibility of that, sir."

"Especially if you gave a favorable recommendation to the D.A.?"

"I'm not promising anything, sir."

"Isn't Elmira a much pleasanter place than Attica?"

"No prison is nice, sir, but from what I hear, Elmira is not as unpleasant as Attica."

"Thank you, Sergeant," I said and turned back to Borovic. "John, you have a simple choice. I'll let you keep your stock, nothing else, so your girls can eat; they're innocent. You walk out of here quietly with Sergeant Palmieri, let him read you the Miranda warning, then you make a statement. Do it, if you wish, in the presence of your personal attorney. Sign all the papers Carter presents you, no fighting. You have ten seconds. After that, I go to work."

Borovic sat tight-lipped, hands clasped between his knees, staring at the floor.

After five seconds I said, "And we'll call it the Borovic speaker." John burst into tears, got up, and walked over to Sergeant Palmieri. "I want to make a statement," he said.

XXIX

Warren did not say one word to me on the drive home. But as soon as we got inside the front door he started crying. "Why, Dad, why did you have to be so cruel?"

I put my arms around my son, my only son, Thelma's son, and held him tight. For the first time in fifteen years I held him close to me. "It's all right, Warren, it's all right," I said. "I wasn't cruel; I was kind. Really."

"Did you see his face, Dad? There was no life left in it."

"I know. But he had killed a man. Kassel was dishonest, a cheat, but he didn't deserve to be murdered. Borovic was trying to cheat his partners, the men who had worked with him to build up their business, their life."

"You could have left things alone, Dad. Borovic could have gotten a good lawyer. With a case as complicated as this, he would have had a good chance of being acquitted."

"That's true, Warren. So let me give you a problem, pose an ethical question; maybe it's even a philosophical question. Borovic's partners are neither angels nor devils. They're all trying to produce a good product at a fair price; to support their families and for reasons of pride and for everything else that drives a human being. Borovic is the chief designer. He has agreed, voluntarily, that all his designs while he is an employee, officer, and stockholder of the company, are the property of the company. That's his function, what he gets paid for. He decides he wants it all and, in order to do this, he must destroy the company and the lives of his partners and their families. Not to mention Hamilcar's employees and their families. Can we agree on these facts so far, Warren?"

"Yes, Dad," in a very small voice.

"He retains an unlikable old man, Walter Kassel, to help him. Kassel is dishonest and tries to steal Borovic's design for himself, breaking his agreement with Borovic. Borovic does not have to kill Kassel; he can accept his small share of the benefits coming to Hamilcar and swallow his pride. He could have said, 'Well, I could have had ten percent of the benefits. I tried to steal one hundred percent and ended up with five percent. That's the penalty for failure, but I'll still eat, my family will eat, and I'll go on.' Did he, Warren?"

"No," Warren said. Whispered.

"No," I echoed. "He decided to commit murder. To kill a man. For what? He made very little extra money that way; the papers were signed and the money allocated. It was pride, wasn't it? What do the Greeks call it?"

"Hubris," Warren said.

"Yeah. His pride was justified; he was a great designer, but . . . So he killed Kassel. If you and I hadn't decided to look into it, he would have gotten away with murder; the police would never have solved this case. In fact, you were the one who got us involved, who told me we had to solve the case. Remember, Warren?"

"I remember, Dad."

"So, suppose I kept my mouth shut. Borovic gets a good lawyer. With whose money? You think Carter Hamilton would not have cut him off the way I did? Don't let those hippie overalls fool you; Carter is a smart businessman. But let's say Borovic has a rich father-in-law, or something. There's a trial. It's in the papers for weeks. His wife has to lock herself in the house. His kids have to leave school, the other kids make life hell for them. Is this what you want?"

"Not really, Dad."

"And if he wins? Where does he go to make a living? Uganda? Definitely not in the hi-fi business; who would dare to have him around? And if he loses? Twenty-five-to-life in Attica? Do you have the faintest idea of what it's like? Someday ask Palmieri, privately. Five years in Elmira is no picnic, but if it's handled properly, and I'll do my part, Borovic and his family will still have a life left; he's young. I had to shock him into the right action, at least what I thought was the right action."

"You succeeded, Dad. I'm just not sure what's the right action anymore."

"That's what I was coming to, Warren. Here's your problem: The clock is turned back. I'm not in Carter's office. I didn't interrupt your analysis. What is your goal? To do right? To maximize the amount of good in the world? To fight evil? To follow the precepts of your religion? I don't care. Sooner or later you have to act. Or to not act. But *no* action is an action, too, a choice that has consequences. So what would you do, Warren? What is your decision?"

He didn't have to think. He looked up at me, even though he's taller than I am. "I would do," he said slowly, "I *hope* I would do, what you did." Then he put his arms around me. For some reason, I was crying, too.

Afterward, when it was time to let go, I poured a little sherry for both of us. "In a few days," I said, "Waxman will be finished with the paperwork. You'll be officially half-owner of Nassau Venture Capital. You could sell it to me, if you wanted to, at fair market value, and do whatever you wanted. But what I'd really like . . . I would be very pleased, Warren, very, if you would take an active interest in the firm. Maybe even on a permanent basis. What do you say, Warren?"

"I want to finish my book, Dad."

"I want you to finish it, too, Warren. And to explain it

to me, some day, whatever I can understand. NVC doesn't require you full time yet, but I need your mind, your backward way of thinking."

"I'll try, Dad."

"Warren," I had never said this before, but it was the time, "Warren, I need you."

"And I need you, Dad," he answered. "Here I am."

I let the moment set on us, these things have their own rhythm and you shouldn't spoil it. Then I smiled, benevolently, as befits the head of a family. "Warren, I have a present for you. You may not know it yet, but someday you will. It's a two-way present, and I'll tell you what it is in about ten years. And I want you to do something for me in return. Don't ask questions; just say yes. Next Sunday night, you and I will have dinner at Iris Guralnik's house."

Warren didn't ask questions. He just said, "Yes."

"We make a good team," I said.

"We make a good family," he corrected.

Also by Herbert Resnicow

The Gold Solution
The Gold Deadline
The Gold Frame
The Gold Curse
Murder Across and Down
The Seventh Crossword
The Crossword Code
The Crossword Legacy
Murder in the Super Bowl (with Fran Tarkenton)